"You Said You Wanted to Look at the Stars."

"I don't want to look at the stars and neither do you," he retorted in a husky voice, molding her body to his. "You know what you want as well as I do."

"Just a minute!" She pulled herself free of his arms. "You've got the wrong idea!"

"Yes, and we both know how I got it, don't we? Now, come here and stop playing hard to get. You've tempted me, and I've taken the bait."

What kind of woman was she? she asked herself. Bracken was right. She *did* want him to make love to her!

BRENDA TRENT

has a life right out of romance. She followed her heart from Virginia to California, where she met and married the man of her dreams. With his encouragement she gave up working to concentrate on another dream: writing. We are proud to present her work in Silhouette Romances.

Dear Reader:

I'd like to take this opportunity to thank you for all your support and encouragement of Silhouette Romances.

Many of you write in regularly, telling us what you like best about Silhouette, which authors are your favorites. This is a tremendous help to us as we strive to publish the best contemporary romances possible.

All the romances from Silhouette Books are for you, so enjoy this book and the many stories to come. I hope you'll continue to share your thoughts with us, and invite you to write to us at the address below:

Karen Solem
Editor-in-Chief
Silhouette Books
P.O. Box 769
New York, N.Y. 10019

BRENDA TRENT

Run from Heartache

Published by Silhouette Books New York

America's Publisher of Contemporary Romance

Other Silhouette Books by Brenda Trent

Rising Star
Winter Dreams
A Stranger's Wife

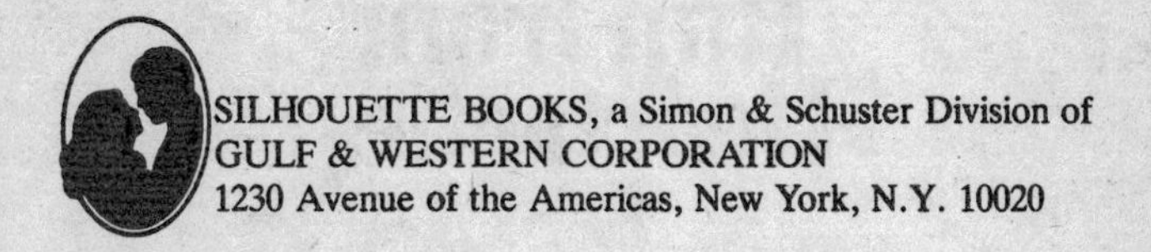

SILHOUETTE BOOKS, a Simon & Schuster Division of
GULF & WESTERN CORPORATION
1230 Avenue of the Americas, New York, N.Y. 10020

Distributed by Pocket Books

ISBN: 0-671-57161-3

First Silhouette Books printing July, 1982

10 9 8 7 6 5 4 3 2 1

Map by Tony Ferrara

America's Publisher of Contemporary Romance

Printed in the U.S.A.

Run from Heartache

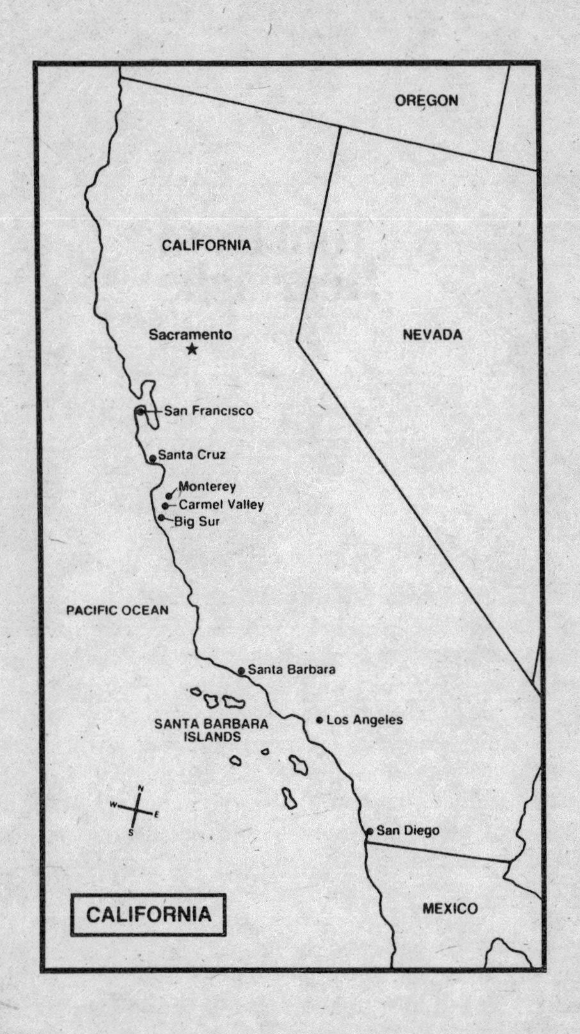
OREGON
CALIFORNIA
Sacramento
NEVADA
San Francisco
Santa Cruz
Monterey
Carmel Valley
Big Sur
PACIFIC OCEAN
Santa Barbara
SANTA BARBARA
ISLANDS
Los Angeles
N
W
E
S
San Diego
CALIFORNIA
MEXICO

Chapter One

Rebecca McCaskie brushed angrily at the tears spilling from her sad blue eyes. She tossed back her head, trying to clear it of agonizing thoughts, and her cap of short, dark, springy curls bounced with the motion. How could Desmond have treated her so abominably? How could he have deceived her with his protestations of love? She had thought she knew him so well. She had made up her mind to share her life with him. A sob rose in her throat and she swallowed hard. She tried to tell herself that she was extremely fortunate that she had seen this side of him before she married him, but that fact didn't lessen her misery.

Clasping the gold band she had chosen for him tightly in her fist, she again wiped at the tears that ran down her cheeks. How it hurt to know that he didn't love her! His words kept ringing in her head. He had spoken cruelly to her; he had taunted her and mocked her. He had said that she didn't know how to be a real woman, how to lose her inhibitions and enjoy life. He had called her a snow princess and told her that he wanted a party girl —something she was too prim and proper ever to be. He had scoffed at her principles and told her he would never marry a woman until he knew that she was suitable in *every* way.

She shoved her foot fiercely down on the gas pedal of the large car, knowing that the mountain road was treacherous and that the cliffs of the Big Sur area plunged to the ocean below, but uncaring of the danger. She was lost to all but the bitter ache in her heart.

Rounding a sharp curve, she suddenly hit an unexpected patch of dense fog. With a gasp of horror, she saw that she was heading directly toward a small car. She twisted the wheel, but seconds later she heard the grinding of metal against metal as the two vehicles met. Her head hit the steering wheel with a thud. She tried to look up to assess the situation, but she felt herself slipping, sinking into a dark void. Far, far away she heard someone open a car door. A hostile voice growled bitter words and Rebecca supposed that they were addressed to her, but she wasn't sure.

"You reckless little imbecile!" A huge hand grasped the hair at the nape of her neck, lifting her head from the steering wheel, and she valiantly tried to focus as she looked into the coldest pair of gray eyes she had ever seen. A strange light glowed in them for just a moment, then there was a look of pure agony as the dark face paled. Rebecca wanted to apologize. She wanted to explain, but her glance drifted over the handsome face and the darkness in her head grew blacker. She heard a soft groan, and then someone—the man? herself?—murmured the name Marissa. Her head hurt and she was too confused to decide who had spoken. Yielding to the soft comfort of the blackness inside her head, she closed her eyes with a sigh of relief.

Rebecca's head was throbbing painfully when she came to. Her eyes opened wide in fright and she glanced nervously around the unfamiliar room. Touching her forehead, she moaned softly, trying to remember where she was. There was an empty bed across from hers, stark and white. When she realized that she was in a hospital room, she felt panic well up inside her. Had she been hurt?

"So, you're finally awake," a deep voice murmured. She looked toward the door and saw a man leaning against the wall, watching her. His face was familiar, and, comforted, she held out her slender hand to him. When she saw him move toward her bed with a panther-like grace, she frowned. What was his name? She was sure she knew his face, but she couldn't find his name anywhere in her mind.

"How do you feel?" he asked brusquely. She sensed from his expression and his tone that he was angry with her, but she couldn't remember why. She must have hurt herself to have landed in the hospital, but how?

"I think I'm all right." But she didn't know, did she? Her uncertain blue eyes met his winter-gray ones. "*Am* I all right?"

"I think so," he replied, with no softening of his tone. "You have a head wound and perhaps a concussion, but no major injuries. Do you feel all right?"

She sighed and raised a hand to her head. Shocked when she touched a bandage, she quickly withdrew her hand. "I have a headache," she murmured.

"Who are you?" he asked sharply, his cold eyes raking over her face demandingly.

Puzzled by his anger, she stared up at him. "Why,

I'm . . . I'm . . ." Who was she? It was the darndest thing, but she couldn't seem to think of her name. It was ridiculous; of course she knew who she was. "I'm . . ." Tears of impotence welled up in her eyes. It was embarrassing and ridiculous, but she simply couldn't remember.

"Well, come on," he prompted impatiently. "Who are you? The hospital will notify your family, and there's the matter of the bill."

She sat up, her head throbbing painfully with the motion, and she looked around for her purse. She didn't see it anywhere. Where could it be?

Putting a restraining hand on her arm, he ordered, "Lie still, or I'll have to get the doctor. Now, don't play games with me. What's your name?"

Confusion showed on her face, and she looked wildly around the room. "Where's my purse? I must have some identification."

His face darkened ominously as he glared at her. "Are you trying to tell me that you don't know who you are? Is that what you mean?"

Helplessly, she shrugged her slim shoulders, her eyes darkening with her distress. "Of course I don't mean that. I know who I am. I must know who I am, but with this headache, I can't seem to think." She massaged her pounding temples. "Oh, where is my purse?"

"What were you running from?" he asked suspiciously, his eyes narrowing menacingly. "You didn't have a purse with you in the car." His voice was suddenly confidential. "Now, you and I know that no woman goes off without her purse. Tell me the truth. I don't have time for silly games, and you have involved me in this whether I want to be or not."

"Oh!" she cried out in irritation. "I'm trying to tell you the truth. Stop bullying me! I don't know who I am right at this moment. I don't know what I was running from.

I . . . I . . ." From the depths of her mind, a name suddenly floated up. She almost grasped it, and then it disappeared. She closed her eyes and struggled to recall it. Was it a name with an M? Mary? Margy? Marissa! That was it! "I think I remember," she murmured, an absurd sense of relief and triumph flooding through her. "I think my name is Marissa."

"No!" he barked savagely, his face blanching. "That's *not* your name! That is my wife's name. You don't even know her."

Clutching the sheet, she sat up straighter. "You don't have to shout," she murmured defensively, mustering all her courage to meet his hard gaze. "I didn't know that. It just came to mind. But I know you, don't I? If you tell me who *you* are, I'm sure I can remember who *I* am."

"You *don't* know me," he stated coldly, crossing his arms and impatiently tapping his fingers on his elbows as he continued to glower at her. "Neither my wife nor I ever saw you before. You crashed your automobile into mine, but I certainly don't know who you are."

She lowered her hands and stared disbelievingly at him. *She had crashed her automobile into his?* "Are you hurt?" she asked hurriedly.

"No. I don't look hurt, do I?" he snapped, his features rigid.

Her eyes skimmed quickly over him. No, he didn't look hurt. In fact, he was almost too good-looking. Dressed in a charcoal vee-necked wool sweater, with thick hair curling over the vee, and black form-fitting jeans, he was enough to take her breath away. He had to be at least six feet tall, his shoulders broad and well defined, his chest tapering down to a slim waist, his legs long and muscular. Her gaze traveled back up to his face with its strong angular jaw, full mouth, and aquiline nose, and to those piercing gray eyes fringed by thick copper lashes. His rich chestnut hair waved slightly, and she was sure that he kept the waves rigidly controlled. Even as she looked at him, he ran a heavy, restraining hand over them.

"Well?" he demanded in a mocking tone.

Lowering her eyes, she swallowed hard and shook her head. "No, you don't look hurt."

"So," his lips curved into a tight smile, "we have an anonymous person here. I've been run into by a mystery lady."

"My car," she said, suddenly inspired. "There must be some identification in it."

His dark brows merged in an intimidating line. Cool gray eyes studied her critically. "I may be a fool, but I believe you really don't remember anything."

She opened her mouth to protest his insinuation that she had been lying, but he spoke again. "The car is rented. It's being checked on now. The doctor didn't know when you would come around." Abruptly turning his back to her, he started toward the door.

She felt the quickened rise and fall of her breathing. She didn't know anyone, not even herself; she didn't want him to leave. "Mr. . . ." she called hesitantly.

He spun on his heel to stare sternly at her, and she blinked back threatening tears. She didn't want to beg him to stay. She didn't even want him to see her vulnerability.

"Yes?"

"Where am I? I mean, where is this hospital?"

"Monterey." He turned away from her for the second time.

"Wait!"

"What is it now?"

"Please," she whispered softly, her eyes pleading, "don't leave me."

A peculiar expression crossed his face briefly, and she saw his jaw muscles twitch as he looked intently at her. Then he shook his head in resignation. "I'll just get the doctor and let him know you're awake," he replied in a less severe voice.

The tears glistened in her eyes as she watched him walk out the door, and she fought for control, clenching her fists in frustration. Who was she? How could she have forgotten her own name? She touched the bandage again. The crash—it must have knocked her senseless. But surely her memory would return. It had to! Where had she been going? What had she been doing? Why didn't she have any identification? She tried desperately hard to remember, but her mind was blank. Staring down at her hands, she noted the absence of rings. And where were her clothes? Perhaps the clue was there.

Glancing nervously at the door, she saw a short, round man dressed in a white jacket enter the room, accompanied by the tall man.

"Hello. I'm Dr. Dickerson. I'm glad to see that you've come around," he said pleasantly, a warm smile on his lined face. "How do you feel?"

"I can't remember who I am," she burst out in a desperate voice, clenching her hands. "I . . . I . . ."

The doctor took one of her hands in his and patted it reassuringly. "I'm sure that's only temporary. Don't worry about it. Sometimes these things happen with a concussion."

"When will I remember?" she asked, her eyes wide with dismay and unhappiness.

He shrugged. "An hour? A day or two? We can learn your name from the car rental agency. Something will trigger your memory, so don't look so devastated. Can you remember the car crash? Do you know where you were going? Can you recall anything at all?"

She inclined her head and chewed on her lower lip as she searched her mind for some shred of information. There was nothing. It was as though she hadn't existed before, and it was terribly frightening. She shook her head helplessly. "I remember Mr. . . . whatever. I remember him looking at me," she said, pointing at the tall man. "He called me Marissa, I think. That's all I remember. Everything went black, and I guess I fainted." She stared at the doctor with stricken eyes. "Oh, this is awful. I just can't remember."

His eyes wide, his bushy brows lowered, the doctor stared up at the other man. "You called her Marissa, Bracken?"

The man gave a short, bitter laugh. "Don't you see the resemblance? The jet black curls, the big blue eyes, the small slim shape? My mind played a trick on me."

Dr. Dickerson nodded solemnly, looking thoughtfully at Bracken for a moment before he looked back at the girl. "Yes, I see the resemblance." His penetrating eyes settled on Bracken again. "Minds do play tricks sometimes. Well, I think it will be best to leave her here overnight while we wait for the information from the car rental agency. That's all right with you, isn't it?" he asked, facing her with friendly, faded blue eyes.

She nodded. What else could she do? Where would she go if the hospital released her?

"By the way," the doctor said, "this is Bracken Bohannon. And we should call you by some name. Do you have any suggestions?"

She shook her head. She had never thought about how really significant a name was, any name. "I don't know," she whispered. How could she know what to call herself when she didn't remember anything? She didn't know the time of the day or the month of the year. She didn't even know what year it was. Suddenly it seemed very important to know those facts. "Is it summer?"

"Your name?" Dr. Dickerson asked, his eyes lighting up as though he had discovered something.

She shook her head again, hating to disappoint him and

feeling foolish. "No," she said apologetically. "I mean, I don't know if that's my name. I want to know what season it is. I'm so warm. Is it summer?"

The light died out in the doctor's eyes. "It's April. Springtime. I thought you had remembered something. Well, Summer will make a nice name anyway. It's my granddaughter's name, and I've always liked it. Why don't we call you Summer until something better surfaces?"

"All right," she murmured in a resigned voice. How awful to be given a name in such a casual way. It was so impersonal, so mechanical. But she did love the summer so. Things were warm and bright. Uncomplicated. Her brow furrowed. It seemed that she had something very important to do in the summer. Very important. But she couldn't recall what it was.

"Well, I have to leave," Bracken announced.

Summer looked at him with wide, frightened eyes. She felt so forlorn at the idea of him leaving. "Thank you for staying with me," she murmured tremulously, feeling her heart race. Of course she couldn't ask him to stay. He didn't even know her, and no doubt his wife, Marissa, was waiting for him at home.

The cool gray eyes focused sharply on her, and his expression softened a little. "It was no trouble. I hope you'll be all right."

He turned away and walked out with the doctor. Summer fought down the urge to call out to him, to ask him to stay with her a little longer. She was being ridiculous; she couldn't understand the frantic beating of her heart as he disappeared from sight. Feeling deserted and miserable, she lay back against the pillow and closed her eyes, realizing she would probably never see him again. She meant nothing to him, of course. She had been only an inconvenience. She felt a terrible sense of aloneness when the door closed behind him. How could she have forgotten everything so completely? She must have relatives. Friends. People who could help her, if only she could remember who they were.

Opening her eyes, she looked around for a mirror. She wasn't even sure what she looked like. Not seeing one, she dropped back on the pillow again. Suddenly considering the far-reaching complications of her situation, she found her eyes filling with tears, which soon began to stream down her face. Sobs caught in her throat, and she rolled over on her side and covered her face with her arm. She felt so helpless, with no past and an uncertain future.

When she heard the rustling sounds of a uniform as a nurse came into the room, she sniffled and tried to stop crying.

"What is it?" the nurse asked. "Can I help you?"

Tears clinging to her long dark lashes, Summer stared up into the woman's face. "I feel so lost. I don't know who I am, and I can't remember a thing about myself. Where will I go from here? What will happen to me?"

"Now, now, you're working yourself into a state for no good reason," the nurse said calmly. "The highway patrolman who investigated the accident is checking on you now. To rent the car you had to show a driver's license. Now stop fretting. Do you want something to drink?"

Summer hadn't thought about a driver's license, but, of course, she had to have one somewhere. The knowledge made her feel a bit better, and she rolled over on her back and propped herself up against the pillows. "What time is it?"

"It's after one. You missed lunch, but I can have a tray sent up for you. I'll bring you a dinner menu later, so you'll have a choice for tonight. Do you want something to drink now, or do you want to wait for the lunch tray?"

"I'll wait," Summer said. "And, nurse, will you get a mirror for me, please?"

"Oh, so you want to look pretty for Bracken Bohannon,

do you?" she teased. "He is a handsome man, isn't he? If I ever have an automobile accident, I hope I run into someone like him."

"I am *not* trying to look pretty for him," Summer protested quickly. She certainly wasn't interested in a married man, though she had to admit that there had been something magnetic about him. "How well do you know him?" she asked, trying to appear casually interested. Unaccountably, her heart pounded at the question, and she licked her lips nervously.

"Bracken Bohannon? Don't you know who he is?" The nurse acted as if it were impossible not to know. "You can't remember anything, can you?"

Summer shook her head. "Who is he?"

"He's a famous novelist. He's very well known, and very wealthy."

"Oh," Summer murmured. The name hadn't meant anything to her, but then, she didn't even know her own name. And maybe she didn't read much. "Where does he live?"

"He lives in Big Sur, where you had the accident. It's about thirty miles from here."

"Do you know his wife?" Summer murmured. She couldn't imagine why her heart fluttered so frantically at the question.

The nurse blinked large green eyes as she looked at Summer. "His wife is dead. She was driving too fast one foggy night—missed a turn and drove right off a cliff. Rumor was she and Bracken had quarreled and she was leaving him. She didn't die right away, so she was here in intensive care for several days. Bracken Bohannon was a tortured man during that time. There was a big write-up in the papers. Makes you wonder, doesn't it?" she mused, shaking her head. "Now, why do you suppose a woman married to him would want to leave him?"

Summer couldn't possibly imagine. Her stomach tensed

at the thought of the tragic story. She was intrigued enough to suppress her own unhappy plight momentarily. "What do people think?" she asked in a small voice.

Tilting her head, the nurse carelessly shrugged one shoulder. "Oh, there are those who say she had her reasons. There was some talk of Bracken having a mistress he loved more than his wife. On the other hand, there was talk that Marissa Bohannon had her share of lovers. Who knows? She was a pretty little thing, and it looked like she had everything a woman could want." The nurse shrugged again. "Oh well, let me find you a mirror. Actually, you look fine, but you know, of course, that your hair had to be cut off in front, don't you?"

Summer quickly raised her hand to feel the bandage again. Tracing the patch across her forehead, she touched the hair behind it. She must look a fright!

She watched as the nurse walked away, then she lay there, barely breathing, waiting for the woman's return. It was several minutes before she was given the hand mirror.

"There," the nurse said soothingly, "not a mark on your face and only three stitches in your head."

Summer stared in shock for a moment at the bandage, which crossed her forehead, taped down to her temples on each side. Then she allowed her eyes to appraise her face. She was actually rather nice looking, she decided after careful scrutiny. Her skin was clear and lovely, her mouth was well shaped, and her eyes were a stunning deep blue, fringed by long sweeping lashes. Her nose was small and attractive, and her hair was naturally curly. She was relieved to know that she looked presentable, but it had done nothing to trigger her memory.

The nurse took the mirror and placed it on the night-stand. "Now, why don't you rest a bit? You should stay in bed, you know. You might be a little dizzy, so if you need to get up, ring for me."

Summer returned the woman's smile and closed her eyes again, feeling as if she could sleep forever.

Later, she was vaguely aware of someone trying to rouse her, but she was too tired to pay much attention. It was much easier just to sleep and to forget. A tray of food was moved into position so she could eat, but Summer was too sleepy. She mumbled her appreciation and drifted back into the numb refuge of sleep.

She turned restlessly in the bed, troubled by nightmares and confusing thoughts. She kept seeing Bracken's face, his gray eyes full of agony; she was troubled by the way he looked at her. And there was another man who kept appearing in her dreams, but all she could see of him was the back of his head. His hair was very blond and straight. Once she saw a dark woman, and she thought the woman was laughing at her; but why? Then she dreamed that she didn't know who she was, or was it a dream? She sensed that someone was staring at her, and her eyes shot open in alarm. Terrified, she sat up in bed, a hand over her mouth, and she looked into Bracken Bohannon's frowning face. She remembered him, and she felt a tremendous sense of relief, even though he watched her with moody, perplexed eyes.

Moving away from the wall he had been leaning against, he approached her bedside with sure, confident strides. "You're all right," he said calmly.

She settled back against the pillow, letting her breath slip slowly from between slightly parted lips. "I dreamed that I didn't know who I was, and now that I'm awake, I still don't know."

"But I do," he stated flatly, his brow furrowed. "You're Ellen Story, and you're twenty-five years old. Though you don't look it, I must say. You live here in Monterey, and you have a bank charge card."

"How do you know?" she questioned.

"The highway patrolman checked with the car rental agency and local police. They're still gathering information, but that's a start. A policeman was here earlier, but you were sleeping."

Ellen Story. Summer turned the name over in her mind, but it didn't trigger anything. It sounded like a nice name, however, and she was comforted by it; it was a beginning, something to give her cause for hope. Surely she could be traced now. She must have relatives. A home. A job.

"Well?" he asked, looking down at her curiously. "Does the name mean anything to you?"

"Ellen Story," she murmured aloud. Did it sound familiar? She wasn't sure. "I don't think so, but maybe when I talk with someone who knows me, it will make all the difference in the world."

"Yes, I suppose so."

"Oh, dear!" she muttered in frustration, gently touching her forehead. "I wish I could remember something!"

"You will. I'm sure it will all come back to you. You must be married. You probably had a fight with your husband and drove away in a huff."

"Married!" she exclaimed, the idea totally foreign to her. "Why do you say that?"

He took a man's gold wedding ring from his pants pocket and held it out to her. "This was clutched in your hand."

So she was married, she told herself, staring at the ring he handed her. She turned it over in her hand and studied it. It seemed to be fairly new and didn't look as though it had been worn much. The design was unique; it looked like a broad, flat gold chain. Married, she thought again, the notion vaguely disconcerting. Funny, she didn't *feel* married, and worse yet, she had no memory of a husband. Her brow wrinkled. Why would she have this wedding band in her hand? Had she divorced him? Was she widowed? She stared at her hands. She wasn't wearing a ring. What had happened to hers? It made her head ache to think about it. In fact, she couldn't bear to think about it. It would just have to come to her. Now that she had a name, at least she had something to work from. Ellen, she thought. It didn't mean anything to her, and she closed her eyes wearily.

"You're tired," she heard Bracken say. "I'll leave and let you rest. It will be dinner time soon."

Her eyes flew open; she didn't want him to leave her again, but she had no right to detain him. He owed her nothing, and he had been more than kind, considering that she had been the one who caused the accident.

"It was good of you to come," she murmured, her eyes on his face. There was a controlled energy in his manner that drew her to him. She knew she had no right to find him so appealing, and she tried to suppress her response. "Will you let me know what the police find out?" she asked, wanting to keep him with her for just a few minutes longer.

"Yes." He nodded and gave her a grudging smile. "I don't know why, but I feel responsible for you. You seem like such a little lost lamb. Twenty-five," he mused. "You don't look a day over twenty-one."

It was funny, but she had thought she looked rather young when she gazed into the mirror. She shrugged and gave a nervous little laugh. "I guess I'll never have to worry about my age."

"At twenty-five you shouldn't give it a thought." He stepped away from the bed. "You're still young. I was thirty last month. I'm bordering on middle age," he said with a grin. "Try not to worry your pretty little head about your predicament. I'm sure it will all work out."

"Thanks," she murmured halfheartedly, laying the wedding band on the table. As she watched him leave, she wished she were as confident as he was. Her lips curved in a smile; he had called her pretty. Her hand rose to her head again, and she grimaced as she touched the bandage. Pretty, indeed! She had forgotten about the bandage. Bracken Bohannon was simply being kind to her, and she had been thrilled by his statement. He was probably remembering his wife. Summer chastized herself for being such a silly girl—woman, she corrected. Twenty-five was certainly old enough to be called a woman!

For some time she lay in bed, fighting confusing thoughts, which were as much about Bracken as about herself. So he had been married and had cheated on his wife. The idea bothered her, and she didn't know why it should, since he didn't mean a thing to her. She was glad when dinner was served and there was something else to occupy her thoughts. The meal, consisting of a salad, a medium-rare steak, a baked potato, and a dish of fruit, was quite good, and she ate it hungrily, focusing her attention on her empty stomach. While she sat up in bed, sipping a second cup of coffee, Dr. Dickerson came in to talk with her.

"How do you feel?" he asked, his faded blue eyes twinkling.

She shrugged. "All right, I think. I still have a bit of a headache, but it hurts less than it did earlier."

"It should be completely gone in two or three days."

"I'm glad to hear that. And will my memory return when the headache leaves?"

He shook his head uncertainly. "Perhaps. Perhaps not. Now that you know who you are, something will probably trigger it."

"Have my relatives been notified?" she asked hastily.

"I have bad news there, I'm afraid." His expression was sympathetic. "We haven't been able to locate any relatives."

"No relatives?" she murmured, a pained look entering her eyes and her heartbeat increasing. How awful to have no one. Well, she thought, trying to take heart, she must have a home, friends who took the place of relatives, a job, some kind of a routine; she would just have to take it from there.

"Let's take a little stroll and see how you feel," the doctor said, looking critically at her. "Before we release you, I want to be sure that you don't suffer dizzy spells."

Summer nodded and slipped to the edge of the bed. She was a little woozy when she first put her feet on the floor, and her legs trembled slightly. After a few steps, however, she began to feel more confident. The headache was persistent and nagging, but it didn't incapacitate her.

"Yes, I think you'll be all right in the morning," the doctor decided, his voice cheerful. "You're doing fine. You can get back into bed, but make an effort to walk around a little later on."

"I will," Summer promised.

Dr. Dickerson patted her hand. "Good. We'll release you tomorrow, but I'll see you in the morning when I make my rounds, if you're still here. Have a good night."

"Thank you," she said, grateful that he was kind and caring. She spent the rest of the evening watching television, walking around her room, and worrying about her loss of memory. What would await her in the morning? It was so frightening not to know about one's own life. She felt stripped of her identity, bereft of her personality. It was terrifying not to know what the past held. And what about the future?

She tried to get a good night's sleep as the doctor had advised, but she was restless, and she slept badly. She woke up several times feeling panicky, and only the thought of Bracken eased her mind. She would imagine his handsome face and his sure, confident manner, and she would be reassured. Then she would think of his wife and his mistress, and she would feel disheartened again. She couldn't understand her preoccupation with him; surely it was only because she knew no one else. She felt greatly relieved when she finally heard the morning nurse enter to check on her.

"I'm awake," she announced. "Good morning."

"Good morning," the plump, gray-haired woman said. "You're the mystery woman, I hear."

"Not anymore," Summer said. "I have a name. Ellen Story."

"Oh? I hadn't heard that, but it's good news. Maybe you can go home today. Breakfast will be served in a few minutes. Do you want to wash up in the bathroom?"

"Yes," Summer said, getting out of bed to walk toward the bathroom. There was a shower, and after stripping off her gown, she turned the spray on and stepped in, being careful not to get her bandage wet. When she had bathed, she dried with a white towel and slipped back into the gown. She was still trying to tie the ties when she left the bathroom. With a gasp she looked up into Bracken Bohannon's face. "I didn't expect you so early!" she cried, clutching at the skimpy gown.

He watched as she hurried back to the bed and climbed under the covers. "Writers are funny people," he said at last. "One never knows when to expect them. Sometimes I write all night and sleep all day, and then again, sometimes it's the other way around. This time, however, I spent the evening checking on you."

"And?" she asked expectantly. She could feel the wild thudding of her heart, and her breathing quickly became labored.

"I didn't learn anything about your family," he said bluntly. "I don't know anything about you. I was wrong. You're not Ellen Story. The police checked with the apartment manager where Ellen recently leased an apartment here in Monterey. She's in Europe somewhere. She rented the car, but you aren't her."

Summer stared at him wide-eyed for a moment. "But

maybe I am," she reasoned, feeling a sudden desolation at having no name again. "Perhaps I was going to the airport when I crashed into you."

He shook his head firmly. "I'm sorry. You aren't Ellen Story."

"But how can you be so sure?" she cried, feeling frantic.

"I'm sure," he said grimly.

"Then who am I?" she demanded. "Who am I? You tell me that!"

Chapter Two

"I don't know," he said, watching her carefully. "But there's no doubt that you aren't Ellen. She has flaming red hair, and even with dye, you couldn't achieve that effect. And she has green eyes. If I remember correctly, and believe me, I do," he murmured, stepping closer to her and staring down into her eyes, "yours are bluer than a summer sky." He shook his head. "Besides, she's five feet, ten inches tall, and you're not an inch over five feet three, if my guess is right. No, you're not Ellen Story."

"Oh, no," she murmured, running a hand along the side of her face. She felt as though she had been set adrift on the ocean again without a sign of land. "What was I doing in the car she rented?"

He didn't answer, but his gaze was speculative.

"No!" she cried suddenly. "You can't think I stole the car! I didn't! I know I didn't do that!" She sat up quickly, stiffening her spine.

"I never said you did," he asserted. "I didn't even think it."

"Well, you—you . . ." She sagged back on the pillow and inadvertently touched the wound on her head. She winced as she looked away from him. "What am I going to do now?" she whispered to no one in particular. "Where will I go?" Her lips trembled slightly, and she fought the urge to give way to tears.

Hearing a tap on the door, she looked up as an officer entered to confirm Bracken's information. "I understand from Mr. Bohannon that you will be staying with him temporarily," the man said in conclusion. "If we get more information, we'll contact you there."

Summer glanced quickly at Bracken. "Staying with you? I don't even know you!"

"Where else would you stay?" he asked in a taunting tone. "Have you another place in mind?"

Her face reddened as she stared from one man to the other, watching as they exchanged glances. Of course, she had no other suggestions.

"Let me speak to her alone," Bracken requested. "I'm sure we can clear this little matter up."

The officer nodded and excused himself. When he had closed the door behind him, Summer turned to Bracken. "Whose idea was this anyway? And why are you willing to take me in?"

His eyes whipped over her momentarily, and his features hardened. "Ungrateful, aren't you? I'm not exactly eager for your company either, but I can't just forget about you and leave you to your uncertain future."

"Don't do me any favors!" she snapped, instantly annoyed by his attitude and the way he had embarrassed her in front of the officer. She hadn't said that she was against the idea of going home with him; she had just wondered why he was making the offer at all. His attitude certainly seemed to be hostile.

Bracken stared coldly at her without replying.

Looking down at her hands, she laced her fingers together and then unlaced them. "Why are you offering to take me in?" she repeated more softly. "I've been nothing but trouble to you." Looking at him from beneath long dark lashes, she waited for his answer.

His lips curved into a half-smile. "Yes, you're right about that, but I've never known a mystery lady before. You bring out the writer in me. Maybe I'll find out that you're worth the trouble. I intend to get to the end of this puzzle." He studied her face with an unfathomable expression in his eyes. "Who knows? You may be my next book."

Summer was annoyed by his admission. "Oh, so you're only concerned about me so that you can write my story. Is that it?" she asked indignantly.

His eyes became solemn for the briefest of moments, and she imagined that she saw pain in them. "Seems like as good a reason as any," he said. "Besides, I've told you, somehow I feel responsible for you."

"You needn't," she retorted, but she was glad when he refused to bicker with her further.

"Get dressed so we can leave," he snapped. "Your clothes are in the closet."

Summer watched as he turned on his heel and stalked from the room. Of course she would go with him; he was a badly needed refuge even though she resented his insolent manner.

While he went to check her out of the hospital, Summer retrieved her clothes from the closet. She had just laid them out on the bed when a woman stepped into the room with a breakfast tray. The food smelled good, and Summer took a few minutes to eat before Bracken returned. Then she began to pull on her clothes.

As she slipped into a demure white blouse, a full dark pleated skirt, nylons, and prim blue shoes, she stared down at the outfit. So this was how she dressed. Not very glamorous, she decided. She laughed lightly at her reflection in the bathroom mirror, and from the recesses of her mind the words of a song came to her, something about a good-time girl, a party girl. She certainly didn't fit the image of a party girl in these clothes, but surely they were hers. And yet the words of the song would not go away, and she was sure that someone had called her a party girl. She shrugged, tired of struggling to make sense of the contradiction.

She started when Bracken tapped on the door and entered. She felt small as he stepped up behind her, his muscled frame towering above her. She felt vulnerable, and for some silly reason her heart began to hammer. She *wanted* to go home with him! She was astonished at the excitement that shot through her at his nearness. It was all so disconcerting, not knowing what kind of personality one had. Had she known love on a moonlit night in the arms of a handsome man, a man like this one? She blushed at the thought, and she was relieved when he spoke, shattering her fantasy.

"Are you ready to go?" he asked, his baritone voice rich, but gruff.

Because of the irritation in his voice, Summer stirred instantly from her musings. "I guess so." When she looked at him again, she wasn't sure she wanted to be thrown on his mercy, no matter how exciting she found him to be. He obviously felt less than thrilled by the whole situation. "There doesn't seem to be anything more I can do. I feel so empty without my purse. Are you sure it wasn't in the car?"

"Positive," he replied curtly.

"How much damage was done to the car?" she wondered suddenly.

"Very little. I suffered most of the damage because of the angle at which you struck me."

"I'm sorry." She frowned. Whatever had prompted her to drive so carelessly? Was she in the habit of doing such things? She shook her head again. She had no answers to her questions, so why did she torture herself with them? She was fortunate to have some place to go under the circumstances, she reminded herself unhappily.

They had started to leave the room when Bracken turned back. "You forgot this," he said, picking up the ring and practically tossing it at her.

Summer caught it, and looked away. As Bracken strode from the room, she hurried to keep up with him. "Where do you live?" she asked to hide her embarrassment at forgetting the wedding band.

"In Big Sur. I have forty isolated acres. I hope you won't mind."

"Mind? No, of course not," she said quickly, averting her eyes again, but the idea was a little frightening. After all, she didn't know this man, regardless of his reputation as an author. Why did he feel responsible for her? Was she really just another book idea to him? Or was it because she looked like his wife?

It irritated her to think she reminded him of his dead wife. If that was the reason he was concerned for her, then she didn't want his interest. "Mr. Bohannon, please don't feel that you're under any obligation to help me. You don't owe me anything. I've been enough trouble to you already. I'm sure I can manage on my own somehow," she said suddenly.

"Call me Bracken," he insisted as they left the hospital and entered the parking lot. "So, you could manage? Have enough money to tide you over, do you?" he asked sarcastically.

"You know I don't have any money," she muttered, glaring up at him.

"Then tell me," his tone was mocking, "what would you

do if I walked off right now and left you here? Where would you go?"

She gritted her teeth, then shrugged helplessly. "Why I would . . . I would—oh, darn!" she sputtered irritably. She didn't have anywhere to go. She didn't know what she would do. "It's really no concern of yours," she snapped, balling her hands into fists as she watched his lips curl into a taunting smile.

"You have a temper," he teased, his face creasing in deep lines of amusement. "I was just curious if you had plans. I don't know what you would do either. So, it seems that I'm stuck with you. I wouldn't turn a dog out without a bone."

"I'm hardly a dog," she said sharply. He had made her angry by forcing her to acknowledge that she was totally dependent on him. She *was* grateful that he was willing to take her in, but she didn't like him throwing the fact in her face. "I would survive without you, I'm sure," she insisted, her tone defiant.

His laughter was deep and low. "I think you would, and Summer, I wasn't comparing you to a dog, though you are snarling like one. You're quite a little tiger—even with that bandage. A little bit of a thing who talks big." His eyes skimmed over her petite form. "Well, let's get on our way," he said coolly. "I have things to do." Grasping her hand, he led her across the parking lot.

Summer was annoyed by the way her heart leapt at his nearness. She admitted to herself that she found him physically appealing, but she didn't really even like the man. She had simply had no choice but to accept his hospitality. Her hand felt like it was on fire as he held it, and she wondered if he noticed how hot it was. He was so very virile and so masculine that he took her breath away. She tried to subdue the feelings of excitement that he evoked within her, but it was a losing battle. She was wildly attracted to him, no matter how she fought against it, and she didn't want to be. Her mind whirled frantically; there had to be some way to find out who she was.

Fleetingly, she considered having her picture put in the paper, but she discarded the idea as much too drastic even for her desperate situation. It was degrading, and it would attract a lot of crank calls. She was sure Bracken would spurn the idea anyway, and she couldn't blame him. Obviously, he lived in Big Sur because he wanted the isolation. She shook her head wearily; she would have to wait for the police to turn up something, and she would have to live with Bracken while she waited.

Escorting her to a Seville parked at the front of the lot, Bracken opened the door for her.

"Your car doesn't seem to be damaged," she commented, impressed by its sleek lines.

"This isn't the one you hit," he said emphatically, helping her get in. "That was my Porsche. It will take awhile for it to be repaired, but I don't drive it much anyway."

"Oh," Summer murmured, falling silent as he got in and drove out of the parking lot. She was lost in her thoughts until they left the city behind and she noticed the magnificent scenery. The area was breathtaking in its beauty, but Summer didn't remember ever having seen it before. She stared out at the blue expanse of the ocean, watching as the waves pounded the rugged shoreline and birds busied themselves among the rocks. Across the highway the cattle were grazing on hillsides covered with wildflowers and tall trees. For a moment she watched a hawk soar against a background of brilliant blue sky.

"Penny for your thoughts," Bracken said, smiling faintly at her.

Turning to look at him, Summer made a wry face. "I'm afraid they aren't even worth a penny. I was just thinking how absolutely gorgeous the countryside is. I don't think I've ever seen anything quite so beautiful, but I don't remember any of it."

"Don't try to remember," he said. "Just enjoy it for now. I think it's the most splendid spot in the world." His eyes sparkled as he surveyed his surroundings.

Summer nodded, but she didn't say anything else. She was seeing a warm side of Bracken that she hadn't expected, and she wanted to savor the moment.

The ribbon of highway unraveled before them as they drove toward the densely wooded area Bracken identified as Big Sur. It seemed to Summer to be an oasis of calm in the middle of civilization. Only one road led in and out of the community, ensuring a minimum of traffic.

"What does the name mean?" Summer asked, finding it a rather curious choice.

"When the Spanish set up the Carmel Mission, they called the wilderness to the south *El Pais Grande del Sur,* the big country to the south. The two local rivers were called *El Rio Grande del Sur,* the big river to the south, and *El Rio Chiquito del Sur,* the little river to the south. Americans eventually shortened the names to the Big Sur and Little Sur Rivers. Big Sur got its name from the Big Sur River."

"It is kind of catchy," Summer agreed after a moment.

Abruptly, Bracken pulled off the main road and stopped the car before a locked gate with a no trespassing sign. He pushed the button of a remote control unit in the car, and the gate slid to one side so they could enter. When they were inside, he pressed the button again and the gate locked behind them. Summer studied him from the corner of her eye as he worked the device. He was ruggedly handsome, and there was something about him, like this country around them, that said he would be controlled by no one. Perhaps his wife had tried to tame him, she mused. She brushed the thought aside. Why was she so concerned with his circumstances when she didn't even know her own?

She gazed at the lush vegetation all around her; the wildflowers made a multicolored carpet beneath the tall redwoods, big leaf maples, pines, and laurels. Summer recognized the orange bush monkey flowers, the reddish-orange Indian paintbrush, the white, blue, and purple colors of the lupine, and the delicate petals of the poppy. Ferns flourished there also, but she wasn't sure of the different varieties. They traveled some distance along a circuitous route to a contemporary house that was invisible from the road. Perched on the side of a hill facing the ocean, it was sheltered by several huge, crooked trees. Summer stared up in wonder at the attractive tri-level structure built of redwood, oak, and stone. She looked at the numerous walls of glass, then at the redwood deck around the two upper levels. As her gaze traveled down to the savage surf pounding the rocks below, she decided that the house was perfect for the virile Bracken Bohannon.

"This is wonderful," she breathed. "I can understand why you want to live here."

"Yes," he mused. "I'd hate to give it up. There's a controversy going on right now. Some outsiders are pushing to make this area a national park, but most of the residents are against it."

"I would think so," she murmured, imagining the tourists who would inevitably flock to the area if it were made into a park.

"There are national forests and state parks here already, but I guess a taste of beauty only makes some people hungry for more." He got out of the car and walked around to her side to open her door. "Welcome to Isolation," he said, watching her step from the car. "This house is the only evidence of civilization for miles around.

I've purposely left the grounds just the way they were when I purchased the property, except for a small plot of land that has a vegetable garden. Wild game still roams the land."

Summer could tell that he was proud of his home, and as she gazed at the grounds, she knew his pride was justified. "It's marvelous," she said. "It's so primitive."

"Yes, it is, but don't be worried about being lonely. I'm sure you won't be here long."

Summer hadn't the vaguest idea why, but his statement hurt her feelings. He seemed suddenly to resent her intrusion. "Of course not," she murmured defensively. "I'm sure the police will discover who I am very soon."

Bracken nodded. "There isn't much to do here, not even a television to watch. Very few people in the area have one. Some people don't even have electricity."

"I don't watch much TV anyway," Summer answered quickly.

Bracken faced her with a strange expression in his eyes. "How do you know that if you can't remember anything?" he asked suspiciously.

She shrugged. She didn't know how she knew. "I don't know, but I'm sure I don't," she said meekly.

Bracken digested her reply, but he made no further comment. "I have a staff here, though I often give them time off," he said finally. "Rose and Harry Ellery. They're visiting their daughter in San Diego now. You have me all to yourself," he added dryly.

Summer's heart beat faster. "I see," she said, unable to account for the shiver that played along her spine. What on earth was wrong with her? She wasn't afraid of Bracken Bohannon. In fact, she mused, she was more afraid of herself. She didn't know what she was capable of, and she was undeniably drawn to the man. She felt the color taint her cheeks, and she heard him laugh.

"Don't worry. I have no plans to ravage that tempting

little body of yours. Not yet," he added coolly. "You're too much of a mystery, in more ways than one. I wouldn't dream of poaching on another man's property."

"I'm nobody's property! Besides, I'm quite sure that I can take care of myself, regardless of what you think. I don't need your reluctant assistance."

"Is that so?" he asked, raising thick brows as he looked down at her. "Well, let's see." Walking up the steps to the front door, which was situated at the second level, he unlocked it and held it open for her.

Belligerently, she flounced inside ahead of him, determined to destroy his image of her as all talk. What did he think she would be afraid of? Who did he think he was? She didn't care if he was rich, famous, and handsome. Those things didn't matter to her. He was no better than she was, even if she *didn't* know who she was.

Suddenly a mammoth red Doberman raced across the room, his long teeth plainly visible. Summer was sure he lunged at her, and she cried out in fright, instinctively turning to Bracken for protection.

Gathering her in his arms, he held her to his muscled body for a moment as he stared down into her eyes. Summer saw an odd look flit across his face briefly, and for a moment she thought that he was going to kiss her. It was an absurd thought, of course. They really didn't care for each other when it came right down to facts. They had been thrown together by circumstances, and it was apparent that they rubbed each other the wrong way, even if Bracken had felt some need to offer her his home. Anyway, her immediate concern was with the dangerous dog. She looked away from Bracken to stare at the animal. It had collapsed in a heap at his feet, and it was trying to get his attention as it pawed at his dark boot.

Embarrassed, Summer stepped out of Bracken's arms. "That was a dirty trick!" she accused. "You knew the dog would do that. Does he bite?"

Bracken bent down to playfully rub the dog's head. "Devil, the dangerous Doberman? Bite? I got him for a watchdog when he was six weeks old. So far, the only person he watches is me. He does bite, however. Pillows, chair legs, shoes, his toys, and sometimes a bedspread, but he has never bitten a human being, so you need have no fear. He's as harmless as a gnat."

"He doesn't look it," Summer sniffed, holding herself rigid.

"You'll grow to love him," Bracken predicted matter-of-factly. "Everyone does."

Summer wasn't at all convinced. She felt sure that he could devour her with one chomp of those massive jaws, and he weighed almost as much as she did, she was sure. Besides, he had made her act like a fool. "Aren't Dobermans vicious?" she demanded.

"Well, well, you do remember something," Bracken said tauntingly. "And, yes, some are vicious, but you have nothing to worry about with Devil," he said, dismissing the animal. "Come on. I'll show you around, then I have to get to work."

Stepping away from the dog, Summer watched it roll over on its back and make a variety of noises as it wiggled on the carpet. She took a deep breath as she followed Bracken out of the room and down some stairs. She had to stifle a gasp when they reached the bottom. The entire lower level was a huge enclosed recreation room. An oval swimming pool shimmering with blue water was in the center, and an assortment of game tables and game boards were placed along the walls. Walking around the pool, Bracken indicated a sauna room.

"Feel free to use these facilities any time," he offered.

"But I don't have a suit," she answered instantly.

He grinned wickedly. "All the better. Let me know when you want to swim."

"I will not!" she retorted angrily before she realized he was baiting her.

He chuckled as he led her back up the stairs and into the living room. Heavy, dark wood beams arched to the ceiling, enhancing the rustic atmosphere of the house. The furniture was a mixture of dark rattan pieces and large, low country couches and chairs.

"It's quite impressive," Summer murmured.

"It's home," he said modestly. "I'm glad it meets with your approval," he added mockingly.

Following him from the living room, Summer noticed a lovely painting on the hall wall. "How beautiful!" she exclaimed.

Bracken turned back to see what had caught her attention. "Yes," he agreed, "it's called 'Wings of the Ocean,' by an artist known as J.J.—Jeff Anderson. He lives in Monterey. I'd like to have more of his works, but they're snatched up as quickly as he completes them."

"I can see why," Summer said, trailing behind him through the rooms on the second floor, including a sunny kitchen and a large many-windowed dining room. Upstairs she was shown the bedrooms and baths, one of which featured a glass-windowed shower and a Jacuzzi. She was shown a pretty bedroom decorated in pastels, but what attracted her attention was the large arched skylight. She couldn't remember ever having seen a skylight in a bedroom before.

Noticing her fascination, Bracken said, "You can have this room." Then he led her down the hall to an L-shaped wing where she was shown a library and his study. She was enthralled with his study; bookshelves rose to the ceiling on two sides of the room, a long desk curving before each of them. A typewriter and several manuscripts were stacked on each desk. A large picture window overlooking the Pacific Ocean took up one entire wall.

"What a wonderful room," she breathed. "And what a stunning view."

"Yes," Bracken agreed. "I spend many hours here, and I like to work in comfort, as well as have something to see. Some days I watch whales and sea lions with my binoculars, and some days I find it relaxing to watch Harry and Rose work down in the garden."

Summer stared down at the large plot of land neatly separated into rows. She hadn't noticed it before.

"Well, I have work to do," he said abruptly, leading her out of the study and back down the hall past a room with a closed door.

"What's in here?" Summer asked innocently. She was unable to miss the harshness in Bracken's voice when he answered her.

"It's a storage room, not that it matters to you. You don't need to see every nook and cranny, for heaven's sake!"

"No, of course not," she said quickly, but his blatant hostility had piqued her curiosity immediately. It was true that she didn't need to see every nook and cranny, but what was so special about a storage room? What was stored in it? Was it something that she shouldn't see? She dismissed her wild thoughts instantly, but still she wondered why Bracken had been so cross with her over such a simple question.

When they were back downstairs, Bracken said, "Maybe tomorrow we'll go into Monterey or Carmel to buy some things for you. In the meantime, I think I have some items you can use. Why don't you put on a pot of coffee while I get them? You'll find everything in plain view."

Summer nodded, then turned toward the kitchen as he left the room. She couldn't help but wonder if Bracken were going to produce some of his dead wife's personal belongings; she didn't know why the thought should bother her, but it did. She put a kettle of water on the stove to heat and took down a jar of instant coffee.

When Bracken came into the kitchen, he had a brush and a comb and a new toothbrush. He also had a huge robe and a man's tee shirt, which were obviously his. "Here," he said, practically shoving the articles at her.

Summer couldn't help but think how ridiculous she would look in the clothes, but she could use the tee shirt for a nightgown, and the robe would come in handy in the morning. "Thank you for your thoughtfulness," she said coolly, matching his attitude. It *had* been considerate of him, even though his brusqueness detracted from the gesture.

Pulling two heavy mugs from the cupboard, Bracken spooned coffee into them while Summer took the kettle off the stove and poured in hot water.

"I'm going to work," he said, a steaming mug in his hand.

Summer nodded. She didn't know what she would do with her time, but after he was gone, she climbed the steps, finding her way through the unfamiliar halls.

She went into her large, pleasant room and walked across to the window. When she opened the draperies, she saw that it, too, had a view of the hills and the ocean. She pulled a chair up to the window and looked out over the grounds and canyons as she sipped her coffee. She saw a long, low building in the distance, and she wondered if Bracken had horses. For some time she sat sipping the dark brew, thinking about the future and about Bracken Bohannon.

Finally draining her cup, she set it down on the bureau and wandered to the full-length mirror to stare at her reflection. The bandage on her forehead made her look ridiculous, and she tugged gingerly at the tape, wanting to see how much damage had been done. There was a nasty bruise and three stitches just above the hairline, but the wound didn't look bad. She was more alarmed about her hair, which was a fright; a large chunk of it was missing right in the front where the bandage had been. Brooding as she stared at it, she decided to find some scissors and see if she couldn't at least even it up a bit.

First she searched the bathrooms, then, having had no luck, she looked in the three other bedrooms. The one next to hers was Bracken's, and she quickly closed the door, afraid that he would think she was snooping if he saw her. The two rooms across the hall were more modest, and one was obviously a rarely used guest room, but there were no scissors in evidence. Going down the L-shaped wing, Summer approached Bracken's study and started to knock on the door. Caught in a moment of indecision, she didn't know whether to bother him or not. He might get angry.

Shrugging, she turned away, walking back down the hall past the room with the closed door. It captured her attention. What better place to look for scissors than in a storage room? she asked herself. And after all, Bracken hadn't told her she couldn't go in, only that she didn't need to. What could it matter? Even as she slowly turned the knob, she felt the hammering of her heart. She realized that her curiosity was the main reason for entering. She had known from Bracken's angry response when she asked about the room that she wasn't free to make use of it, no matter how she tried to delude herself. Still, what could it hurt?

Slipping inside the silent room without a sound, Summer looked around in amazement before closing the door. Apparently this had been Bracken's wife's room, a kind of private haven. There were old dolls and mementos sitting about on the desk and divan. A flute sat on a table by a music stand; the book was still open to a page of music. A bookcase filled with poetry books had a number of pictures of Bracken and Marissa on it. Her pulse racing, Summer crept closer to stare at the small dark woman. Marissa did look somewhat like Summer, but she had a spoiled, pampered look about her.

Summer bent to study a picture of Marissa laughing up into Bracken's face while he held her possessively to his long body. She had just reached out a slender hand to pick up the photograph when she heard the door slam behind her. Guiltily, she jumped as if she had been shot. She knew it was Bracken. Who else could it be? But she couldn't muster the courage to turn and face him. The atmosphere became tension-charged as she stood there, frozen before the picture of the two lovers.

She counted the heavy steps as Bracken strode across the room to where she stood. She almost cried out as fingers of steel bit into the soft flesh of her upper arm as he spun her around, nearly knocking her off balance.

"What do you think you're doing?" he roared, glaring down at her with fiery eyes. "Why are you sneaking around in this room?"

Summer pried his cruel fingers off her arm and backed away from him, frightened of his fury. "I was looking for some scissors. I wasn't sneaking around," she murmured defensively, rubbing her arm where his fingers had cut off the circulation. She stiffened her spine and tilted her head proudly. She hadn't done anything to warrant this treatment.

"There are no scissors in here! Get out! And don't come in here again!"

Tears rose to Summer's eyes, and she blinked them back; she'd die before she would let him see a single tear fall. "I haven't hurt your shrine to your dead wife," she proclaimed bitterly. "You don't need to carry on as though I desecrated something sacred. You're behaving like a madman."

"Don't talk about my wife," he ordered coldly. "Just

get out!" He grasped her arm again and this time she was unable to loosen his grip.

"I'm going!" she cried. "But keep your hands off me!"

His hand pressing painfully into her arm, he dragged her toward the door.

When they were back in the hall, he closed the door with a slam. Summer jerked away from him and stalked downstairs to the kitchen, hating him for his treatment of her, and hating him for the room he kept as a memorial to his wife. There had been no reason for him to behave so deplorably. If his marriage had been the stormy affair the nurse had described, why did he keep the room just the way Marissa had left it, and why had he reacted so fiercely to Summer's intrusion? Had he realized too late how much his wife meant to him, or was he consumed with guilt over his part in the accident?

Sitting down heavily on a kitchen chair, Summer stared out a sliding glass door. She realized with a rush of feeling that she was jealous of a dead woman. Shoving the chair back, she flounced into the living room and dropped down into an overstuffed recliner. She hated being dependent on Bracken Bohannon. She'd like to leave him to live unhappily forever after here in his dream house. She wished she knew who she was. She wouldn't stay here a minute longer. She would go away and never look back. But wishing was futile. She knew only too well that she had nowhere else to go.

Chapter Three

Summer had been sitting in the living room for only a few minutes when Bracken entered, holding a pair of scissors. "Here," he said coolly. "Next time you want something, try asking."

"I went up to your study, but you were working, and I didn't want to disturb you," she replied, her voice icy. "I didn't think you would be happy about it."

"I wouldn't have been," he retorted. Then he turned on his heel and left.

Not even so much as an apology, Summer fumed. She grabbed the scissors from the table where he had laid them and stormed back up the stairs to the bathroom at the end of the hall. Stepping up to the mirror over the basin, she began to trim the hair over her forehead, trying to give the butchered patch some shape. She apparently didn't know a thing about cutting hair, because the pieces she trimmed just kept getting shorter and more ragged.

"Rats!" she muttered as she snipped away. Soon there would be very little left. She finally managed to make the front look reasonably decent, but she had to trim the back to get it to blend in and then the sides. Her eyes widened in horror as she finished. She looked like a young boy, with no hair to speak of and huge blue eyes. Turning on the tap, she dunked her head, trying to be careful of her stitches. After towel-drying the shaggy fringe, she fluffed it into wispy strands, staring at the hint of curl she had left. Her hair *was* terribly short, but after the initial shock, she decided that it was rather attractive even so.

Having finished her venture, she wandered back downstairs and looked in the cupboards, trying to find something for lunch. The pantry and the refrigerator were well stocked, and Summer boldly decided to test her culinary talents, or lack of them. She had no idea why, but as she scanned the contents of the refrigerator, Mexican food automatically came to mind. Why Mexican food? she wondered.

Shrugging aside the new and confusing riddle, she began to gather the contents for *enchiladas rojas*. She was happy to find all the ingredients for the rich red sauce she instinctively knew she cooked superbly. She put the beef in a pan to simmer and hunted for a pot to cook the rice in. For the next half hour she was almost content as she busied herself in the kitchen. She refused to acknowledge the questions that continued to bother her, and she began to hum a happy tune. To her dismay, it was a song about a party girl. She didn't want to think about that either. Resorting to whistling, she jumped when Devil came racing into the room as though on command.

He seemed satisfied to wag his stub of a tail in her direction, but she kept a watchful eye on him as she worked. The arrangement lasted until Devil grew tired of it and vanished.

When the food was ready, Summer placed the *enchiladas,* rice, beans, and a fresh green salad on a plate; then found a tray to carry it on. She had finally cooled down over the incident in Marissa's room, and she sampled the lunch before taking it up to Bracken. It was delicious, as she had somehow known it would be. Making a sign of triumph with her forefinger and thumb, she picked up the tray and walked carefully up the steps. The meal looked lovely, and she had complemented it with a glass of iced tea. She was very proud of finding something that she could do well, and she was hoping against hope that Bracken would be pleased. Standing outside the door, she waited for the sound of typing to cease before she knocked hesitantly.

"What now?" Bracken snapped.

Summer opened the door a crack and stuck her head inside, determined to keep her temper, though his tart question made it difficult. "I made lunch. Do you want to eat?"

Bracken turned cool gray eyes toward her and suddenly he laughed, deep and low.

"What's so funny?" she demanded, opening the door wide and glaring at him.

"What happened to your hair?" he asked, an amused smile lingering on his lips.

Holding the tray in one hand, she raised the other to her hair. "Why? What's wrong with it?"

"Nothing, I suppose," he said more civilly, traces of laughter still glinting in his eyes. "You look like a wide-eyed boy with it all chopped off like that."

She lifted her chin proudly. "It was already chopped off in the front from the accident, so something had to be done with it. Don't look at it if you don't like it!"

His smile faded. "Come on in, Summer. Let's see what kind of cook you are."

She was suddenly furious. Slamming the tray down on the nearest surface, she turned on her heel and fled from the room. She was sure that she heard Bracken chuckling as she hurried down the steps, and she hated him for it.

Returning to the kitchen, she ate her own lunch in silence, no longer relishing the tasty dishes. When she had finished, she began to wash the dishes by hand, though there was a dishwasher. Banging pots and pans around in the sink lessened her anger a bit, and when she was through with the chore she went to her room.

Quietly closing the door behind her, she solemnly promised herself that she wouldn't stay in Bracken Bohannon's home any longer than was absolutely necessary. She *had* to find out who she was. There must be some way to trigger her sluggish memory. She sat down in the comfortable blue chair by the window and thought, trying to picture the blond man's face in her mind, but nothing surfaced. Then she tried thinking of places, names, streets, but there was only emptiness. She even went through the letters of the alphabet, hoping something would surface. But her exercises proved futile; her mind remained shut to the past. Sighing in frustration, she went to the bed and lay down on top of the covers. Wearily, she closed her eyes.

It was much later that she became aware of the tapping on her door. Knowing that it was Bracken and still angry with him, she pretended to be asleep.

"Summer," he called. "Summer!" Hearing no answer, he opened the door and stepped inside. "I didn't realize you were resting," he said, looking at her evenly. "I thought you were sulking."

"I am not sulking," she said tartly, staring at him with smoldering blue eyes, "and I doubt if you would have cared even if you *had* known I was resting."

Bracken watched her for a moment, then crossed the

room with long strides, stopping at her bedside. "You're still pouting about your hair," he drawled with a half-smile.

"I'm not!" she snapped. "I don't care what you think about anything. I think it looks quite all right, and that's all that counts. Your opinion doesn't matter in the least."

"No?" he murmured, seating himself on the bedside. Summer rolled away, turning her back to him. She felt the caress of his hand as he reached out to touch her hair, running his fingers gently through the wispy strands. Her heartbeats increased at once, and she felt strangely breathless. She wanted to slap his hand away, but it felt good to have him toy with her hair; she was comforted by his touch.

That feeling rapidly gave way to excitement as he turned her toward him. Slowly, he traced the line of her lips with a finger, then, before she realized his intention, he bent his head and placed firm, warm lips against hers. Summer twisted once, meaning to pull free of his embrace, but he gathered her to his hard body, and the taste of his lips on hers was much too sweet. She found her traitorous arms winding around his neck as the kiss deepened into a tantalizing caress. She moaned as he stretched out beside her on the bed, drawing her body nearer so that she could not resist him. His fingers spread over her back in widening circles, causing tingling sensations on her skin. The kiss intensified ever so slowly, then Bracken's lips sought her throat, leaving her gasping with the aftereffects of the passionate kiss. Summer's heart raced as his lips trailed to the collar of her demure blouse. Then his expert hands unbuttoned the buttons as his searching lips continued their quest. She felt herself responding to him totally. A small panicky sensation rose in her, and she knew she must stop him, no matter how much she wanted him to quench the fire growing inside her.

"Bracken," she murmured, and to her surprise the word

came out as a husky caress. "Bracken," she tried again with a little more conviction.

At that moment she heard a noise in the hall, and she jerked away from him. "Mr. Bohannon, are you here?" a female voice called out.

"Blast!" Bracken muttered, moving away from Summer. "Straighten your clothes," he ordered, glaring at her as he stood up and saw to his own.

Giving her only a moment to restore order to her person, he strode to the door and called out, "In here, Rose."

A small woman with frizzy gray hair and active hands stepped into the doorway, her dark, lively eyes widening as she saw Summer.

"We got back early, and we wanted to let you know we're home," she said, tugging at the necklace around her thin neck. "When I couldn't find you in the study and the Porsche was missing, I thought maybe you were out." She spoke to Bracken, but looked only at Summer.

"We have a guest, Rose," Bracken remarked blandly in response to her questioning gaze. "Summer, come here."

Resenting his commanding tone, Summer walked slowly to the door, self-consciously smoothing down her skirt.

"Rose, our houseguest, Summer. She's had an accident, and she'll be staying with us while she convalesces."

Rose looked the girl up and down suspiciously, as much as saying that she looked perfectly healthy, but she replied, "Yes, sir. Will you be wanting dinner tonight?"

"Yes."

"Fine. I'll see to it."

Summer stared after the woman as she walked away. She didn't want to look at Bracken's face. She was ashamed of the way she had fallen into his arms, and she knew he didn't realize that she had been trying to put an end to the lovemaking when Rose had called out. She was sure he thought that she had been going to give as much as he wanted to take. She felt her cheeks heat up at the thought; apparently she *was* a party girl, just as the song that kept playing in her mind seemed to indicate. To fall into a stranger's arms after knowing him two days! Had she no scruples at all?

"We'll continue this at a later time, Summer," she heard Bracken murmur, and she raised her eyes to his. "I think we've just learned something about you."

Summer opened her mouth to protest, to try to explain, but what was there to say? She stood in frustrated silence while Bracken left, closing the door behind him. Then, suddenly, the door swung open again.

"By the way, thanks. It was good. The meal, too."

"Go to the devil!" she snapped, and he shut the door on her words with a laugh.

Walking back to the window, Summer slumped down into the chair. Oh, if only she could remember something! Who was she? Did she have a husband waiting somewhere, searching for her, loving her? Regardless of the fact that she had been holding a man's wedding ring, she couldn't make herself believe that she was married. Still, it *was* possible, wasn't it? The thought made her behavior seem even more shameful, and she pressed her trembling fingers to her lips. She had felt so natural in Bracken's arms. She had wanted his loving. She turned to look at the bed where they had so recently been in each other's arms, and she couldn't bear the sight of it.

Striding to the door, she jerked it open and hurried to the living room. She almost ran into an elderly, gray-haired man who looked at her with soft brown eyes. Something about those brown eyes caused her to gasp. A memory from the past was rapidly working its way up to her consciousness, and she waited breathlessly for it to take form.

"Is something wrong, Miss?" the old man asked, and

the memory evaporated as quickly as it had started to appear.

"Miss?" the man questioned again, causing Summer to nervously smooth down the wispy strands of her dark hair.

"I'm all right," she said, trying to appear more cheerful. "You must be Harry."

"Yep." He smiled at her. "And you must be the houseguest the missus spoke about." His eyes swept appreciatively over her. "Shouldn't you be resting? I understood that you'd had some sort of accident."

She gingerly raised a finger to her head. "Actually, I crashed into Bracken's car with mine. I bumped my head." As he stood before her, his face full of concern, there was something in his brown eyes that touched her heart. She certainly seemed to look for comfort from men, and she wondered why. Did she have a father somewhere with brown eyes like those? She realized she was staring at him, and she murmured, "To tell the truth, I've lost my memory. I can't seem to recall a thing."

He shook his head sympathetically. "Now, don't you fret about it, Miss. I've heard of such cases." His sympathy brought tears to shine brilliantly in her eyes. Seeing them, he patted her shoulder clumsily. "There, there. I'll just go and get Mr. Bohannon."

"No, please," she murmured quickly, "there's no need."

His kind eyes searched her face with open curiosity. "No? Well, then, how about a cup of nice, hot coffee? Rose is making some now. Want me to get you a cup?"

"I'll get it," Summer said, smiling slightly at him. "Thank you." She walked toward the kitchen and entered the open archway. Rose's sharp eyes focused on her at once, and Summer felt a little intimidated until she saw the woman smile.

"Can I get something for you, Miss?"

Hearing a noise behind her, Summer whirled around to see Devil galloping across the room, a large bone in his mouth.

"Down, Devil," Rose called out when she saw the fear in Summer's eyes. "He won't hurt you, Miss," Rose said reassuringly. "He's bringing you his bone. He's a real lover, that dog. I brought that soup bone home from my daughter Nora's house, and already he's wanting to give it to you."

As Summer watched, Devil dropped the bone on the floor in front of her, barely missing her shoe. She had to smile at the animal, and she tentatively reached down to pat his head. In response, he panted and jumped around excitedly before picking up his treasure and thundering away again. He seemed to know that he had made a friend of Summer.

"Harry said you were making fresh coffee," Summer told Rose. "May I have a cup?"

"Sure you can." Rose reached into the cupboard for a mug.

"I'll do it," Summer said quickly, hating to inconvenience the woman when she had obviously started to prepare dinner. "And please call me Summer."

Rose looked doubtful for a moment. "Perhaps it would be better if I called you Miss . . . Miss . . . what is your last name?"

Summer giggled nervously. "I don't know. I'm afraid I'm suffering from amnesia. Summer was the name the doctor gave me, and that's all there is."

Rose looked stunned for a moment. "Heavens above," she murmured, shaking her head. "You poor child. How did it happen?"

Summer explained about the accident, and she was touched by Rose's sympathy.

"Now, don't you worry about a thing," the woman said, nodding her head. "Mr. Bohannon will get to the bottom of this. He's real smart and the first thing you know, he'll have it all sorted out, and you'll be somebody again, as sure as you're standing there. You'll be able to leave here and go on with your life."

Summer couldn't understand the depression she felt at hearing those last words. Leaving here would mean leaving Bracken and perhaps returning to a husband. She brushed the thought aside; it might be a long, long time before that happened.

"So you don't have a stitch of clothing but what you've got on," Rose said, stroking her chin thoughtfully. "Now, let me think a minute. Why, I'm willing to bet that you and me wear just about the same size. You come on with me, and let's see what we can find."

"But aren't you supposed to be cooking dinner?" Summer asked, not wanting to get Rose in trouble with Bracken.

Rose made a wry face. "Mr. Bohannon is writing. He won't budge from that room until I go up and knock. Forgets he even has to eat sometimes. He's not demanding, not like Mrs. Bo—" Rose stopped abruptly and paused for a moment before amending the sentence. "He won't care when I serve dinner."

Summer wondered about Rose's comment. Had she intended to say that Mrs. Bohannon had been demanding? Even as selfish and pampered as she had appeared in the picture? Summer knew that she had wanted to hear those things, and she chastised herself for thinking such thoughts. What in the world was wrong with her? She didn't seem to be a very nice person, at least when it came to Bracken's dead wife.

"What was she like?" Summer blurted out, unable to stop herself.

"Who?" Rose asked, leading the way up the steps and down the hall to the bedroom across from Bracken's.

"Marissa Bohannon."

Rose shook her head warningly. "Mr. Bohannon doesn't like her name mentioned," she whispered sharply. "No sir, he doesn't. He gets angry, and he's a man without a conscience when he's angry. You'd best not be worrying about the late Mrs. Bohannon."

Summer sighed disappointedly. She would love not to worry about the late Mrs. Bohannon, but somehow she sensed that the woman would play an important part in her future, and she would need to know all she could about her.

Walking over to a closet, Rose pulled out several items. "Here we go," she said proudly. "This caftan will fit you for sure. It could fit almost anyone, and it's kind of pretty, don't you think?"

Summer fingered the billowing, green garment, noting the soft pale green flowers against the darker green background. "Oh, it's lovely, but I can't take your nicest clothes. Don't you have something you don't wear?"

Rose held up several other beautiful dresses. "I have plenty," she said. "Me and Harry don't do much except visit with Nora and look at each other here at Isolation. There's not much else to do, except maybe go to a movie or drive into Monterey once in a while. But we like it here. Anyway, I buy these clothes and don't wear half of them." She took a pair of pale blue slacks off a hanger. "I imagine you could fit into these. Might do them some good. My shape isn't anything to brag about," she complained, indicating her thin frame.

Summer took the two items and several blouses that she was sure would fit and thanked Rose before returning to her own room. When she tried the clothes on, she was pleased to see that they fit reasonably well; the caftan was quite lovely, and it softened her boyish haircut. Dressed in it, she walked back down to the kitchen and offered to help Rose with dinner.

"Oh, no," Rose replied. "I can't let you do work. You're a guest."

"But I want to," Summer pleaded. "I need to keep busy, unless, of course, you don't want me in your kitchen." Somewhere in her mind the slogan about too many cooks spoiling the broth surfaced. She seemed to be filled with disjointed clichés, bits of songs, phrases that didn't tie in with anything, and faces that didn't have names.

"I don't mind about that," Rose said quickly, smiling at the girl. "But if Mr. Bohannon protests, you be sure and tell him that it was your idea."

Summer smiled. She was sure Bracken didn't care what she did. And she didn't want to have to tell him anything; she just wanted to stay out of his way from now on. "Is he very hard to work for?" Summer asked.

Rose looked at her sharply with her severe, dark eyes, but Summer was no longer intimidated by them, sure now that Rose had a heart of gold. "He's been real moody for the past year. It's hard to know what will set him off. He broods about . . . things."

"Has Marissa been dead a year?"

"Almost to the day," Rose replied. "Her accident happened a year ago yesterday."

Suddenly Rose bent her gray head, busily slicing potatoes, and Summer looked at her curiously before she realized that Bracken had walked up behind them.

"Didn't expect you to come out of your study so soon, Mr. Bo," Rose said brightly, deftly finishing off one potato and picking up another.

Bracken thrust his hands deep into the pockets of his brown jeans as he leaned against the counter in front of the two women. Summer's eyes strayed to his broad chest clothed in the beige vee-necked sweater, and again she thought how good-looking he was.

"I wondered how your trip was, Rose," Bracken said, but Summer didn't think he was really very interested in Rose's trip. His eyes were raking over her, taking in every detail of the lovely green caftan. Foolishly, she held her breath, waiting for him to comment on it, but he said nothing to her.

"It was real nice. Nora sends her greetings. She's finished school now, you know. She's got her job waiting for her—going to be an oceanographer, you know. She's done real well, too. We're proud as peacocks at how she's turned out."

"You have every right to be," Bracken agreed, his eyes searching Summer's face. Looking her up and down again, he almost seemed to resent how lovely she looked in the green gown.

Summer blushed under his scrutiny and kept her eyes on Rose's hands as the woman worked. Why didn't he just go away? He knew he was making her uncomfortable, and apparently that was his intention. She wondered if he thought she had dressed up just for him. But hadn't she? she asked herself with sudden dismay. Hadn't she been concerned about what he would think of her from the moment she saw him? She wished she had never been on that road where she had hit his car. But it was too late for wishes now, she thought unhappily.

"How long before dinner?" Bracken asked.

"About another hour," Rose told him. "I'm fixing some lobsters we brought back with us. How's that?"

"Fine. Then I'll go back up and do a little more work."

Rose nodded, and Summer looked up as Bracken walked out.

"I guess he's making an effort to show his manners since we have a guest in the house," Rose commented pensively.

Summer didn't think that was the way things were at all,

but then, she didn't know what Bracken had in mind. She didn't say anything as she watched Rose put the dish of scalloped potatoes in the oven and turn back toward the sink. "You can fix the salad if you want to," the woman said.

Opening the refrigerator door, Summer gladly turned to the task.

Summer had just finished setting the dining room table when Harry walked into the room with Bracken. He looked at the four place settings with unconcealed surprise in his brown eyes. Saying nothing, Bracken sat down at the end of the table, but Harry hurried into the kitchen. In a minute he walked back in with Rose.

Unruffled, Rose went to the table and picked up two of the place settings. "Harry and I eat in the kitchen. Always have," she said with a small explanatory smile. "We'll leave you and Mr. Bohannon to enjoy each other's company."

"Oh," Summer murmured. She had been looking forward to Rose and Harry's companionship. She didn't want to have dinner alone with Bracken, but there was nothing else she could do. She certainly couldn't ask to eat in the kitchen with Rose and Harry. She looked over at Bracken and saw that his glance was amused. Darn his arrogance! she thought, as she settled in the chair before the remaining plate.

Rose deftly served them and then disappeared into the kitchen. Summer stared at the dishes the housekeeper had placed on the table; the food did look delicious, and she hadn't enjoyed her lunch very much.

"Wine?" Bracken asked, and Summer glanced up at him quickly.

"Yes, I suppose so," she said, holding up her glass.

He poured her a generous amount, and she tasted it

cautiously. It was quite good, and she took a long swallow. Bracken watched her with barely contained amusement as he took a sip from his own glass.

"Go ahead and try the food," he prompted.

Self-consciously, Summer did as he instructed. The scalloped potatoes had a tangy cheese sauce, which Summer found quite tasty, and she thought the lobster dipped in butter was delicious. She gave her attention to the food; as a result, dinner and the cheesecake with cherries that followed were eaten in almost total silence. Summer couldn't think of anything to keep the conversation going, and Bracken didn't even make the effort. She was surprised when he invited her out on the deck to view the stars after they had finished the meal.

"All right," she agreed, following him to the glass patio doors. As soon as he had closed the doors behind them, he pulled Summer into his arms.

She resisted, placing her hands against his chest. "You said you wanted to look at the stars," she said, glancing around in the total darkeness. Down below she could hear the chirping of crickets and an old bullfrog calling out to his lady love.

"I don't want to look at the stars and neither do you," he retorted in a husky voice, pulling her hands down so that he could mold her body to his. "You know what you want as well as I do."

So! He *did* think she would give him anything he wanted to take! Or worse yet, he thought she wanted him to make love to her! "Just a minute, Mr. Bohannon," she said as severely as she could. "I'm afraid you've gotten the wrong idea." She pulled herself free of his arms.

"Yes, and we both know how I got that idea, don't we? Now, come here and stop playing hard to get."

"I'm not playing hard to get!" she protested indignantly. "I know you think that . . . that . . ."

"Yes, I do," he said bluntly. "And I want the same

thing you want, so you can dispense with the pure-and-proper guise. You've tempted me, and I've taken the bait."

Suddenly Summer reached out and slapped his face. "You're wrong!" she cried, and before he could recover, she escaped into the house, running up the steps on flying feet. She might have gotten carried away when she was in his arms in the bedroom, but she wouldn't allow him to degrade her because of one moment of indiscretion. Stepping into her room, she quickly shut the door and leaned against it. What kind of woman was she? She raised trembling hands to her hot face. Bracken had been right. She had wanted nothing more than to be in his arms. She *had* wanted Bracken Bohannon to make love to her!

Chapter Four

Something disturbed Summer as she lay in bed dozing. She opened her eyes with a start, wondering what had awakened her. Then she heard Devil whining; he seemed to be pawing at her door. For a moment she contemplated letting him in, although she didn't know for what purpose. It was only seconds later that she heard Bracken's sharp command.

"Quiet, Devil!"

The dog became silent immediately, and Summer heard a knock on her door. "Are you awake?" Bracken demanded coolly.

"Yes," she answered, gathering the covers around her slender body. Her hair was sure to be a fright, sticking up all over her head. She had slept in the huge tee shirt and she looked ridiculous and lost in it.

Last night came to mind with a rush, and she was sure Bracken would mention it; she would just have to face the music, whatever the tune.

Opening the door, Bracken stepped into the room, his eyes scanning Summer's sleepy form. "Rose is cooking breakfast. Do you want to eat now, or shall I tell her you'll be down later?"

"What time is it?" Summer asked, frowning a little.

"Almost eight."

"I'll get up."

"I'm taking you shopping this morning," he announced. "It's our only chance to do it today. I have too many plans for later in the day. There's a party at the Andersons' house, and while I don't care very much for parties, I should attend this one."

"A party at the painter's house?" Summer questioned, feeling a little breathless. Her hand rose to her hair, and she toyed with the wispy strands. "I'll have to do something with my hair."

Cool gray eyes focused sharply on her. "Who said you're going?"

A flood of red rushed to her cheeks. "Well, you—well, you said you were taking me shopping, and then you mentioned the party. I assumed that—Oh, never mind," she snapped. "I didn't want to go with you anyway."

The piercing eyes skimmed over her as she clutched the covers to her. "I'll take you."

"No," she insisted petulantly, raising her chin. "I don't want to go." She'd be darned if she would go with him now when he obviously hadn't intended to take her. She didn't want to spend any more time with him than she had to. She had no right to get involved with him anyway. Oh, who was she kidding? She *did* want to go with him, of course, but she certainly wouldn't let him know that.

"Stop being childish," he muttered. "You will go. We'll stop by Dr. Dickerson's office today and have him look at that head of yours. Then we'll pick up a few things for you from the shops."

Still pouting, Summer shrugged. "Rose gave me some

clothes. There's no need for you to bother taking me shopping. I've already been enough trouble to you."

"Get up and get dressed. We'll need to get you something new to wear to the party." He inhaled sharply and let the breath hiss through his lips. "You're a contrary little thing. You probably drove your husband nuts with your behavior."

"I didn't!" she cried suddenly, the picture of an angry blond-haired man surfacing and vanishing just as quickly. She fought to find the image again, but it was gone.

"You didn't what?" he asked, his eyes narrowing dangerously. "Did you remember that you have a husband?"

Her eyes met his defiantly. "No!" she insisted. "I don't think I'm married at all." And for some reason she couldn't fathom, she really didn't think so. But who was the blond man she had seen?

"Then who did the ring belong to?"

"I don't know!" she retorted, her voice shrill and angry. "If I knew, do you think I'd be here in your house? Do you think I *like* being here with you snarling and snapping and insisting and demanding and accusing and—"

"All right. All right," he said less harshly, silencing her with his hand. He smoothed down his wavy chestnut hair. "This whole thing is just so bloody frustrating."

"You don't know what frustrating is," she cried, glaring at him. "Your life hasn't changed. You're not the one trying to find some kind of identity. What do you know about frustrating? You're not at the mercy of someone who doesn't want you!"

He shoved his hands into his pockets and stared at her with moody gray eyes. "Summer, it isn't that I don't *want* you. You see, there are just so many things involved—oh, forget it. Get dressed and come on down to breakfast. I want to go into town before the morning is gone."

"Don't go to any trouble on my account," she insisted,

still angry with him. "You don't need to take me to the party."

He frowned as he glared down at her. "All right. All right. I *want* to take you to the party. Does that assuage your pride?"

She chewed on her lip, thinking. It didn't assuage her pride, but she did want to go with him. "No, but I'll go," she finally said.

"So," he mocked, "you'll deign to go with me. Well, thank you very much for your kindness." Turning away from her, he strode toward the door.

"Bracken," she called after him, "there's no need to go shopping. I can wear that caftan Rose lent me. It looked nice, didn't you think?"

Half turning, he looked back over his shoulder, letting his eyes rake over her. "Are you fishing for a compliment now?"

"Oh, get out!" she spat. "A compliment wouldn't mean anything coming from you anyway!"

He laughed aloud as he watched her display of anger, but he still insisted on taking her to the store. "I want to select a dress for you," he said.

"I can select my own dress," she replied tartly. "And besides, I'm already in your debt. I don't want you to buy clothes for me when I already have something I can wear."

"I *want* to," he said in exasperation.

"I have no way to pay you back," she murmured, hating the fact that she was so dependent on him.

"Can you type?"

Her brow furrowed. "I don't know. I suppose I can. Most people can type, can't they?"

"Good. Then you can work for your board and clothes. I usually prefer to type my own manuscripts, right down to the final copy, because I'm always altering scenes, but you can help with some of the typing. I'm behind right now anyway. I haven't gotten my usual number of pages done the last two days."

"And I suppose you blame me?" she snapped.

"Who else?" he called over his shoulder as he left the room.

Summer watched as he closed the door behind him, fuming inside at his insolence. It wasn't until she climbed out of bed that she thought again of last night, and she realized that Bracken hadn't mentioned it at all.

She showered in the lavish bath at the end of the hall, marveling at the view outside the generous fixed panes of tinted glass. It was almost like showering outdoors, for the stall was glass on three sides. Several tall plants sat at each end, adding to the outdoor atmosphere. Summer looked out at the trees and canyons below, then at the surf pounding the rugged shoreline. The view was magnificent, and she almost thought she could smell the saltwater. She stood beneath the sharp spray as long as she dared, then stepped out. After drying with a thick towel, she combed her hair, shaping her short, black curls with her hand.

Returning to the bedroom, she slipped into the blue slacks Rose had given her. They were a snug fit, but they clung to her curves attractively. She pulled a long-sleeved blue blouse from the hanger and put it on. Admiring the outfit in the mirror, she decided that she looked quite appealing. Rose had good taste, and Summer was fortunate in both the fit and the color. She had a sudden longing for makeup and she told herself that she would at least buy some lipstick when she and Bracken shopped.

After she had slipped her feet into her one pair of shoes, she hurried downstairs to the dining room. She gave a small start of surprise when Devil galloped over to her, but she quickly saw that he was simply making her another offering when a tennis ball dropped down on her shoe. The dog stood watching her, apparently waiting for her to pick up the ball. But when she bent down to retrieve it, he hastily snapped it up, completely covering the object with his mouth. Summer decided to let him have it, and she straightened to find Bracken watching her with thoughtful eyes.

"Ready to eat?" he asked.

She nodded, realizing for the first time that she was hungry.

"Rose," Bracken called, and in a moment the woman came into the dining room.

"Morning, Summer. Will bacon and eggs be all right this morning? Mr. Bohannon has the very same thing almost every single day of the year," she grumbled.

If Summer hadn't already seen through the woman's gruff act, she might have been intimidated by it. Instead, she smiled. "That sounds good." She looked up at Bracken as Rose retreated, and she was embarrassed by the way his eyes scanned her figure. Averting her face, she slipped into the nearest chair and stared out the window overlooking the grounds.

Saying nothing, Bracken took the chair nearest hers. Darn, she thought frustratedly, why couldn't he sit at the end of the table, or across from her? Why was he always so provocatively close?

It was only seconds later that Rose entered with two plates heaped with bacon, eggs, and toast. "Juice?" she asked Summer. "Coffee?"

"Yes, please. Both." Summer's eyes met Bracken's, and she saw him watching her speculatively.

"You have a healthy appetite for such a little thing," he drawled.

"Oh? Am I eating too much?" she asked with asperity.

A mocking grin shaped his lips. "I didn't say that. I didn't say that at all. I was just wondering if that shapely little figure of yours could hold up for many more years with an appetite like that."

"Well, I wouldn't worry too much about it if I were you," she said. "I won't be around for you to see."

Bracken laughed softly. "No, I don't suppose you will." Picking up his fork, he turned his attention totally to his meal.

Seething inside, Summer did the same, but she felt a fleeting feeling of unhappiness at the thought of never seeing Bracken again.

When they had finished breakfast, they got in the car for the trip down the winding road from Bracken's home. Isolation was certainly well named, Summer concluded, looking around her. It was the only house in the vicinity, and the woods seemed to close in on it when one got only a little distance from it.

Turning onto the main highway, they drove the thirty miles to Monterey. Their first stop was Dr. Dickerson's office, and Summer was surprised to find that Bracken's name opened all kinds of doors for them. She didn't have an appointment, but she had to wait only a few minutes to see the doctor.

When he examined her head wound, he said he wanted the stitches left in for a few more days, but he told her that the wound was healing quite nicely. In reply to his questions about headaches, Summer told him that they were all gone. Unfortunately, when he asked about her memory, she had to tell him that it hadn't improved. He murmured a few encouraging words to her and told her to come back in a few days. Summer wasn't at all comforted by his gentle words, but there was nothing she could do.

She was glad when they left his office and headed for the stores. The shopping expedition took most of the morning. Bracken, contrary to his casual appearance, was a very shrewd shopper. Summer modeled several evening dresses for him, but it wasn't until she slipped into a soft apricot calf-length dress of eyelet lace that Bracken was satisfied.

Summer had to agree with his choice when she turned to stare at her image in the mirror. She was amazed that she could look so pretty; the pale color set off her olive skin and caused the wispy cap of curls to look delicate and feminine. Her blue eyes seemed very large and innocent, and she thought she needed only some lip color and small earrings to look quite attractive.

"Do you like it?" Bracken asked as she whirled around to face him. She hadn't realized that he had come up behind her, and she bumped into him. He steadied her with a practiced hand, and once again she saw the peculiar look in his eyes. His tone, however, was mocking when he spoke.

"Careful," he warned. "You don't need to throw yourself into my arms."

"I'm sorry," she replied. "I didn't know you were right behind me." She felt her senses run wild at the nearness of him as she looked up into those cool gray eyes. Her gaze lowered to her arm, and she saw that he was stroking it lightly with his thumb. Her eyes met his again, and she almost imagined that he was bending to kiss her. Of course it was a stupid thought.

"How about some shoes?" he asked. "You can't wear the blue ones."

"No," she breathed, sorry that the spell had been shattered. "I don't suppose I can."

Moving smoothly away from her, he shook his head. "Certainly not with that dress."

They decided on three-inch backless heels in an apricot shade a little deeper than the dress. Summer had her doubts about the shoes, even though she assumed that they were just the kind a party girl might wear. She seemed to have a bit of difficulty walking in them, but she didn't want Bracken to know that. Taking a few uncertain steps, she tried to avoid his perceptive gaze.

"What's wrong?" he asked. "Don't you like them?"

"Yes, of course," she said, not wanting to disappoint him.

"After all," he murmured suggestively, his eyes bright with promise, "I don't want to break my neck bending down to dance with you."

The mere thought of him holding her in his arms, moving with her to a slow melody, so inflamed Summer's senses that she couldn't think of a response.

"Select a couple of casual dresses, some jeans for roughing it, a bathing suit, and whatever other personal items you need," Bracken said. "You'll need some other shoes, too. I'll be back in half an hour. I have some shopping to do myself."

"I couldn't possibly ask you to buy so many things," she said.

Bracken surveyed her for a moment. "You pick them out, or I will." He turned to a rack of clothes.

"I'll do it," she said quickly, placing a hand on his arm.

"Good. I'll be back in thirty minutes."

Summer nodded, and she was surprised to feel the now familiar panicky sensation as she watched Bracken stroll from the store. The thought of never seeing him again was almost unbearable. She made her selections hurriedly, giving the most attention to a bathing suit. She decided on a pretty scarlet one that she thought would please Bracken, then she sat down in a chair, staring out the window and waiting for him to return. The uneasy feeling didn't leave her until Bracken walked in the door, as he had promised, half an hour later.

Summer and Bracken had lunch in town, and by the time they returned to Isolation, they had time only for a snack before they dressed for the party. Summer had no time to break in the high heels, and she was a bit apprehensive about wearing them. Bracken urged her to hurry with her dressing, and she was ready by six. It would take them some time to get to the Andersons' home.

Summer sucked in her breath at the sight of Bracken when he knocked at her door. Dressed in a severe European style dark brown gabardine suit with pleated trousers, he was every inch the virile male. The green and brown striped shirt he wore seemed to have been made for him. Summer supposed that his longish, thick, rich chestnut hair had been rigidly styled with a heavy hand, the only indication of discipline visible in this magnetic man. She caught the faint aroma of his aftershave as he moved toward her.

"Don't you remember me?" he questioned in a teasing voice. "Bracken Bohannon, your host, salvation, and escort for the evening."

A faint pink tainted Summer's cheeks. "Yes, of course, I remember you."

"The way you were staring, I thought that what memory you had had failed you. Are you ready, or would you rather look at me all night?"

Summer straightened at once, her blue eyes blazing. "I don't find you appealing enough to look at all night," she snapped. "I'm ready."

Bracken gave a low, sexy laugh. "I'm sorry to hear that. I thought it might prove interesting if you looked at me long enough."

Summer grasped the light wrap and the small purse she had purchased. "Let's go. We don't want to be late."

She walked to the steps and carefully made her way down them; she certainly didn't want to trip while he watched.

Following close behind, Bracken opened the front door for her. "Stay, Devil!" he commanded when the red Doberman came bounding up to them. The animal slunk away immediately, and Summer felt sorry for him.

"Where does he sleep?" she asked.

"His bed is in the den. He isn't mistreated, I can assure you."

No, Summer mused. She didn't think that he would be since it was apparent that Bracken loved the animal. Still, she felt sorry for him, even though Rose and Harry were in the house. He had seemed so crestfallen at being left behind.

The ride to the party was quite pleasant, but Summer felt butterflies in her stomach when Bracken pulled up in front of the lovely Spanish-style house. "I don't have a last name," she cried suddenly. "I need a last name. What if someone asks personal questions about me?"

Bracken didn't seem concerned. "Improvise. It'll be fun. Look at it as a game."

Annoyed that he didn't take her worries seriously, Summer glared at him with icy blue eyes. "That's fine for you to say, Bracken. You're not the one without a name." Even as she spoke, a thought suddenly occurred to her. She would use *his* name! Why not? He had told her to improvise. She would say that she was a relative of his, a cousin. Immediately sighing with relief at her ingenuity, she smiled as she stepped from the car when he opened the door. Yes, it could be fun to improvise at that.

They were greeted by an immaculate butler and shown into a beautiful living room decorated with dark Spanish-style furniture. There were a number of guests present, and soft music was playing in the background. A stunning dark-haired couple stepped forward to greet them. Summer noticed that the woman was expecting and radiant with the glow that often accompanies pregnancy.

"Good evening, Bracken," the man said, extending a hand. "I'm so glad you came. I know your aversion to gatherings like this. You've met my wife, Janine."

The tall woman smiled warmly, and Summer thought she noticed a charming blush coloring her cheeks.

Summer felt a ridiculous twinge of jealousy at the smile on Bracken's lips. "Anyone who had met your wife would surely remember," he said. "She's much too beautiful to forget. How are you, Janine?" Turning to Summer, he said, "Summer, I'd like you to meet our host and hostess, Jeff and Janine Anderson. Jeff is the painter, J.J., who did the painting you admired yesterday."

"How do you do?" Jeff asked. Summer held out her hand, and he took it warmly.

"Summer Bohannon," she said, stressing the last name. She didn't need to turn to see the flash of surprise that crossed Bracken's face. It was apparent for a moment only, but Summer knew she had gotten even with him for his earlier lack of concern.

"Oh, are you two related? Or married?" Janine asked, her lovely eyes widening in surprise.

"No, I wouldn't marry him," Summer said with a taunting smile, having fun just as Bracken had suggested. "Bracken is my cousin, and he wouldn't even be that if I'd had any choice in the matter. I'm just staying with him for a while."

It had been much easier than she thought to improvise, and she enjoyed the obvious discomfort Bracken was experiencing. The next time she was worried, she was sure that he would be more helpful. The butterflies that had fluttered in her stomach settled down, and she smiled mischievously at him.

"Let me introduce you two to a few of our guests and get you a drink," Jeff offered, his teeth a flash of white when he smiled. "Sweetheart, will you see to our other guests?" he murmured to Janine.

Summer and Bracken were introduced to several people prominent in the art world, but Summer wasn't familiar with any of their names. She requested the same drink that Bracken asked for, and she was surprised when the first fiery drink of vodka burned down her throat. She coughed and turned away, but she couldn't miss the amused, puzzled look on Bracken's handsome face.

When Jeff excused himself, Bracken bent his head to

whisper, "When I said improvise, I certainly didn't expect you to use the name Bohannon. You've caused quite a stir. I'm not known to have any living relatives, and now I've produced you."

Summer smiled tauntingly at him. "It will make a wonderful story, won't it?"

She laughed aloud when he glowered at her. The laughter died in her throat when a tall, long-legged young woman with shimmering brown hair walked jauntily toward them.

"Bracken, love, where have you been keeping yourself? I expected you to call me last week." Her eyes raked over Summer and dismissed her. Putting long-nailed fingers on Bracken's sleeve, she stroked the material. "You've been neglecting me for some old book again," she said in a sulky voice, looking coyly at him.

There was a twinkle in his eyes as he looked into the woman's attractive face. "Some *new* book, Darlene," he said with a smile. He turned to Summer. "Darlene Draper, this is Summer, Summer Bohannon, my, ah, cousin."

The angry spark that had danced briefly in Darlene's green eyes died as she looked coldly at Summer. "How do you do, Sunni, is it?" Darlene's arm slid possessively around Bracken's waist. "I didn't know you had any relatives. You've never mentioned any, darling."

"You never asked me about any—darling," Bracken replied.

Summer winced at the endearment. No doubt this was the mistress who had driven Marissa to despair, Summer mused, and she could certainly understand why. The two of them seemed quite attracted to each other, and their relationship was obviously one of long standing.

"It's Summer," she said in a tight little voice.

"What?" Darlene asked annoyedly.

"My name is Summer, not Sunni," Summer repeated more loudly, irritated that Bracken hadn't corrected the woman and grateful that she had any name at all.

Darlene laughed in a low, husky voice. "I don't care what we call you, honey, as long as it's cousin, and not a kissing one."

"She's definitely not that," Bracken said emphatically, looking obliquely at Summer.

The admission angered Summer, and she raised her head defiantly. What had he meant by that? It was a deliberate slap in the face. After all, they had certainly kissed. Well, she would make sure that there weren't any kisses in the future. He had been the one to make the advances, not her, but she would thwart any others he felt inclined to make!

"Are you staying with Bracken?" Darlene asked.

"Only for a short time while I convalesce. I've had an accident, or I wouldn't stay there at all," Summer replied sharply.

"I see." Darlene began to fawn over Bracken, leaning against him suggestively, her voice a low hum as she chatted with him, ignoring Summer. "Dance with me, Bracken," she insisted plaintively.

Bracken made a motion to resist. "I have to keep an eye on Summer."

"You do not!" Summer retorted haughtily. "I can take care of myself!"

"See, darling," Darlene drawled. "Come on, dance with me."

Summer watched as the woman led Bracken toward the center of the floor. In seconds she was wrapped firmly in his arms while Summer stood by, silently aching inside. When she could no longer stand the sight of them, her eyes swept around the room, meeting those of a good-looking blond man across the way. For a moment something about his blond hair triggered her memory, and, unconsciously, she stared boldly at him, willing her faulty memory to give her some satisfaction. The sensation, however, was fleeting, and she couldn't connect it to anything.

The man smiled at her, and realizing that she had been staring, she smiled sheepishly back. Her gaze continued to move around the room, and she was once again unable to miss seeing Bracken holding Darlene in his arms as they twirled about the dance floor. Slow anger burned in the bottom of Summer's stomach, and she looked back at the blond man. He stood up and hesitantly smiled at her again. Annoyed with Bracken, Summer decided to show him that she didn't need his kisses or his attention. She gave the man a brilliant, encouraging smile. In a moment, he had joined her.

He was of medium height with intense blue eyes, and again Summer had the funny feeling that he reminded her of someone, but she didn't have time to try to piece the puzzle together before he spoke to her.

"Are you taken this evening?" he asked with a grin. "Or may I have this dance?"

"I'm definitely not taken this evening, and I would love to dance," she told him. She looked around for Bracken to see if he were watching her, but Darlene had captured all his attention; he seemed to have forgotten Summer altogether.

"I'm Larry Simmons," her partner informed her.

"Summer Bohannon, Bracken's cousin," Summer said, trying to keep her eyes on Larry. They seemed to be drawn continually to Bracken and Darlene.

"Bracken Bohannon, the novelist?" Larry inquired, his thin brows arched.

"Yes. Do you know his work?" Summer was interested that Bracken's name could cause a stir even in the midst of other famous people.

"Doesn't everyone?" Larry asked. "I read his books as soon as they come out. Don't you?"

"Actually, I don't," she murmured. "I don't read much," she hastened to explain, not knowing if she were telling a lie or not.

"I see," he said, twirling her to the music. "What *do* you do?"

"I've just finished school." She was improvising, but somehow the line smacked of the truth to her, and she wondered if there were any basis for it. Somewhere in the back of her mind the names of textbooks struggled to surface, and she concentrated fiercely on them, but she couldn't quite focus on them. When Larry said something more to her, she had to ask him to repeat it.

"I said, do you have a job?"

"I'll get a job when I've finished convalescing. I had an accident, you see." She indicated the bruise, which was still prominent on her forehead.

"I hope you weren't seriously injured."

"No," she said curtly, unwilling to encourage the topic. "And what do you do?"

"I've just finished school, too. I'm a sculptor. Oh, I'm not known," he added quickly, seeing her inquisitive look. "I have an inheritance, a small one, and I've always wanted to live in an area like this."

"Yes, it is beautiful," Summer agreed. Larry spun her around again, and she almost stumbled in the tall heels. Feeling her miss a step, he clasped her possessively to him.

"Are you all right?" he asked, staring down into her eyes.

"Yes." Embarrassed, she looked around to see if anyone else had noticed her clumsiness, and she caught Bracken's gaze. She was astonished at the anger she saw there. What on earth was wrong with him? Who was he angry with? It couldn't possibly be her. After all, he didn't care what she did as long as it didn't inconvenience him.

Looking back at Larry, she smiled deliberately. When the song ended, he asked her to share another number, and she accepted readily.

The tempo picked up this time, and for some reason the term party girl rushed to her mind with the rapid beat. Kicking off the tall heels, she whirled and twisted with Larry, laughing gaily. The fact that Bracken was watching her only caused her to flirt more openly. Larry responded eagerly, and she laughed up into his smiling face as though he were the only man in the room.

She wasn't even aware that Bracken, her shoes in hand, had stepped up beside her until fingers of steel clamped down on her arm.

"You've just gotten out of the hospital," he growled. "Sit down. You've danced enough."

Humiliated by his command, Summer looked up into Larry's eyes, ignoring Bracken's stormy glare. "I feel fine," she insisted. "I don't need you to tell me when I've had enough. I'm just getting started." She lowered her gaze, staring pointedly at the fingers grasping her arm.

"I said you've danced enough," he hissed, towering over her. "I'm responsible for you, and I insist that you sit down."

Summer shook her head stubbornly, trying to free herself from his grip. "Go worry about your girl friend," she replied tartly.

Glaring meaningfully at Larry, Bracken snapped, "If you will excuse us, please, I'll see to my stubborn little cousin."

"Certainly, Mr. Bohannon." Larry's reply came instantly, and Summer burned with fury that he would abandon her so willingly. He almost bowed in his eagerness to please the other man.

Bracken shoved her shoes into her hand. "Put these back on."

Summer was furious, but she saw that they were beginning to attract attention, and, allowing Bracken to support her, she reached down and slipped the heels on. The music had changed to a slow, haunting melody, and Bracken pulled her roughly into his arms.

"What are you trying to prove?" he demanded.

"I don't know what you mean," she whispered, frowning as she looked up at him. "Didn't we come here to have a good time?"

"We did not! I came here because it was expected of me, and you came because I agreed to bring you, an obvious mistake. I didn't anticipate you throwing yourself at the first man who looked at you." His cool gray eyes probed her startled blue ones. "But then, maybe that's the real you. Maybe *that's* the reason your husband's ring was in your hand."

Summer was caught off guard for a moment. "I don't even know if I have a husband," she insisted, stung by his biting words. "The ring could have been—"

"What?" he growled. "It was a man's wedding band."

"So?" she retorted defensively. "Is that evidence that I'm married? Maybe my husband died or we divorced or it was my father's ring," she exclaimed, finding the possibility that it was her father's ring the most agreeable prospect.

"I hardly think that it was your father's. It must be fairly new, and I doubt that you would be running around with your father's ring anyway. No, from the way you were clutching that ring, it had something to do with a man—and I don't mean your father. I'm sure of that."

"Well, good for you!" she cried. "So what?"

"So if you're a cheating wife, I won't be the one to help you."

"I'm not a cheating wife!" she insisted. "Don't judge me by *your* wife's standards!"

His hands tightened on her until she thought he was

trying to crush her. "Don't mention my wife," he hissed. Summer was alarmed by the dangerous glint in his eyes. She knew he was furious, but then, so was she.

"Stop it! You're hurting me. No one asked you to be my bodyguard."

"No one asked, but, unfortunately, I find myself in that position until we can find out who you are. Then I'll be more than happy to let you go. For now, conduct yourself with some decorum."

She tried to pull free of his arms, but she was his captive. "There's no reason for you to concern yourself."

"Ahh, but there is. You've given yourself my name, and you're here with me. That makes you my responsibility."

The song ended, and Bracken's arm encircled Summer's waist, forcing her to walk with him to the couch. Pulling her down beside him, he placed a restraining arm about her shoulders. She was angered by his behavior, but even in her anger, she felt her senses reel at the nearness of him. If only he didn't see her as a problem that needed a solution. Even if he didn't, she asked herself, what then? Perhaps she really was another man's wife. The thought was too depressing to think about, and Summer pushed it deep into her subconscious.

Looking around the room, Summer wondered where Darlene had gone; she didn't see the tall woman anywhere. Only a short time later Bracken decided to leave, and, taking Summer firmly by the hand, he thanked their host and hostess for a pleasant evening and led her to the car.

He was strangely silent on the return trip, and, following his cue, Summer said nothing. A full moon graced the night sky, and the stars twinkled brightly. Summer couldn't help thinking dreamily that it was a wonderful evening for romance. Shaking the thought from her mind, she told herself that she would be glad when they reached Isolation so she could go to her room and get in bed—

alone. She hated to be so near Bracken; he caused all kinds of crazy ideas to come to her mind.

When Bracken stopped the car, she opened the door herself and hurried up the walk. To her dismay, she found the door locked, and she had to wait for Bracken to unlock it. Then she rushed in ahead of him and ran up the steps. She was almost to the top when she lost one of her shoes. As the shoe tumbled down the stairs, Summer missed the step; she felt herself falling backward, only to be caught by hands of steel.

"Don't be in such an all-fired hurry to escape me, and you won't break your silly neck," Bracken growled. "It seems to me that you already have enough problems."

Whisking Summer up in his arms, he walked up the few remaining steps with her firmly in his embrace. Breathless, she tried to look anywhere but at his attractive features. She hoped he couldn't feel the wild beating of her heart against his chest. She expected him to put her down in the hall, but she was mistaken.

Looking down at her with strangely glowing eyes, Bracken carried her into her room, kicking the door shut behind him. The yellow of the round moon shimmered brightly through the skylight, casting a golden glow over the room. Bracken didn't turn on a light. His arms tightly about Summer, he carried her to the bed and gently laid her down, slipping off her other shoe as he did so.

Summer nervously moistened her full lower lip with her tongue. He was so disturbingly near that she felt giddy with anticipation. Breathlessly, she watched him as he stretched out by her on the bed. She knew she should order him out of her room, but she wanted him to stay with her. She could see his profile in the moonlight as his lips descended to hers, and she trembled slightly as he gathered her fiercely to him.

Feeling the suppressed energy in his careful touch, she experienced a primitive and dangerous excitement. His lips caressed hers passionately, and she was powerless to do other than yield to his touch. As the fire flared inside her, she responded with abandon. Her heart was racing when he finally ended the kiss. He stared down into her eyes for a moment before his lips traced a path down her pulsating throat, then caressed the exposed, upper curve of her breast.

Summer had no idea how much she knew about love-making, but she knew without a doubt that she wanted this man's exciting touch. A fire was burning out of control inside her, threatening to consume her with its wild blaze. Bracken slid a hand under her back to unzip her dress, and Summer gasped slightly as he slid the dress from her body. His lips sought her shoulders, and she shivered under their light touch. She was barely aware that he was undressing her. She knew that she must stop him, but she was weak with wanting him.

"You're lovely," he murmured huskily, easing from the bed to slip out of his suit. Summer's heart seemed to be pounding in her throat when she watched him lower his muscled body to her bed once more. She held out her arms, and he slipped into them, crushing her to his hard chest. She had no thoughts of past or future as he stretched out over her. There was no time to devote to a possible husband in her background or to the shameless way she was behaving. Her desire for this man was paramount.

"My beautiful, beautiful, mystery woman," he murmured into her ear. "I don't know what you were running from or who you belong to, but I can't resist you. You're too tempting to turn away from."

His mouth closed possessively over hers, and his hand cupped her breast, his thumb teasing her nipple into hard awareness. Summer wanted him. She wanted him desperately, but as she felt the warmth of his body against hers, something went wrong. Suddenly she felt panicky. She couldn't go through with it. Giving a half-sob, she pushed at Bracken with all her strength. She didn't even know this man! What was she doing here in this bed with him? A picture of the blond man surfaced, and she almost saw his face clearly before the flash of memory faded.

"Desmond!" she cried hoarsely. "Desmond!"

Bracken's body stiffened against hers, and she could feel his anger permeate the room. "Damn you," he muttered vilely. "You cheating little tease!" Pulling away from her abruptly, he moved off the bed, grabbed up his clothes, taking only a minute to step into his slacks before stalking out of the room, and closed the door loudly behind him.

The sound of the door slamming went through Summer like a rifle shot. She shuddered as she lay there in the glow of the full moon, staring up at the skylight, seeing the mocking wink of the stars. What had she done? Who was Desmond? *Was* she married?

She put her hands to her eyes and shook her head slowly as the tears began to trickle down her cheeks. What must Bracken think of her now? How could she have behaved so brazenly with him? She didn't know herself at all. What kind of woman was she? She tried and tried to find the face of the blond man in the recesses of her memory again, but it was lost to her. Like something evil, his face would taunt her at the most unexpected times, then vanish completely when she was desperate to see it. The name Desmond, however, played over and over again in her ears as the long night slowly stretched into a dreary morning.

Chapter Five

It seemed that Summer had just fallen asleep when she rolled over in bed and opened her eyes to daylight. Restlessly, she stared about the room, then awakened abruptly. She was naked, chilled, and lying on top of the covers. The events of the past night rushed to her mind with a flood of shame. How would she ever face Bracken again? How could she face herself? Had there been some truth to his statement about her being a cheating wife? Hadn't she been more than willing, eager, in fact, to go to bed with him?

Her cheeks flamed scarlet. Wasn't it only because the face of the blond man had flashed across her mind that she had ended their passionate lovemaking? Or had she actually realized what she was doing? No, she had been on the verge of giving herself to him. There could be no denying that. She certainly hadn't thought of waiting until she had *his* wedding ring clutched in her hand, had she?

And to have called out another man's name at that

moment! It was too awful to dwell on. She should just get up, put on the clothes she arrived in, and leave Isolation forever. But where would she go? What would she do? Well, she might not be given a choice this morning. Bracken had been so enraged when he stormed out of her room last night that he might turn her out of his house today. And she couldn't blame him! She couldn't blame him if he never spoke to her again!

Wearily, she crawled out of bed and trailed to the shower. The passionate way she had gone into Bracken's strong arms, lying beside him without a stitch on, caused her to flush anew. What had gotten into her? Was she that kind of girl?

A nagging thought played persistently at the back of her mind. Hadn't she felt a surge of remorse at her behavior when it came right down to the moment of commitment last night? Hadn't she come to her senses in the nick of time? Had it only been because she saw Desmond's face? Desmond. He had a name now, but nothing else. What was he to her? Could he possibly be her husband? Of course he could, she thought despairingly. And where was he? Had she been running away from him when she had the accident?

The more she struggled with the facts, the more confused she became. Her head began to hurt, and she knew it would do no good to puzzle over and over the situation. She stepped into the shower and let it pelt her body as she looked out over the grounds below and the blue ocean beyond. This country was truly gorgeous. Did she have a home around here somewhere? In Monterey perhaps. Monterey. Monterey. It sounded familiar to her, but then, she had been taken to the hospital there, and she and Bracken had been there since. Where had she been going when she had the accident? Home to Desmond?

No! No! her heart cried. He couldn't be her husband. Not when she so desperately wanted Bracken Bohannon.

Oh no! She realized suddenly, she was in love with the man. How had it happened so swiftly? Her head throbbed painfully at the thought, and she knew she couldn't face it. It was too confusing. Why did it have to be *his* car she had hit? He had complicated things so terribly.

She bathed quickly and walked back into her room to dress in new green slacks and a long-sleeved apple-green blouse. She looked fresh and vibrant in the outfit, and she slipped her feet into the loafers she had purchased. Drawing a deep breath, she strode determinedly out into the hall and down the stairs, but she was shaking all the while, and she had to fight against the urge to run back to her room. She had to face Bracken and get it over with, but how?

The confrontation wasn't delayed; she met him head-on when she turned the corner at the bottom of the stairs.

"Oh," she gasped, trying to avoid his gaze as he collided with her, grasping her by her shoulders to steady her. As quickly as he had braced her, he released her.

"Good morning," he said coolly. "You're just in time for breakfast."

"Fine," she murmured, trying to maintain a manner as aloof as his. Only a fool could have missed seeing the fury just below the appearance of indifference on his face.

He turned on his heel, and Summer followed behind him to the dining room. She wanted to apologize to him for last night, but what could she say? Sighing wearily, she decided that the less she said, the better. She would just have to wait and see how he reacted to her presence. They seated themselves at the table, and it didn't take her long to see how he would respond to her. Picking up the newspaper, he behaved as though she were another piece of furniture, but Summer noted the twitching of his jaw muscle with dismay. He was angry with her all right, and she didn't blame him.

Seconds later, Rose came into the room. "Good morning," she said in a noncommittal tone.

Summer looked up ruefully and met Rose's dark, troubled gaze. The woman frowned and nodded in Bracken's direction as if to say "beware of him today," but Summer needed no warning. And what was more, she knew the reason for his surly behavior. Rose set the breakfast plates down before them, and Summer picked at her food halfheartedly.

Bracken ate, but he kept one eye on the paper, and he didn't even attempt to make conversation with Summer. When he had drunk the last swallow of his coffee, he stood up. Involuntarily, Summer's eyes raised to meet his icy stare.

"If you've finished playing with your breakfast, we'll go upstairs and get to work. You *are* ready to type today, are you not?"

Caught unprepared, Summer could only nod. Scrambling up from her chair, she walked ahead of Bracken. She was aware of his gaze on her as they made their way up the stairs, but there was no way to avoid it. Holding her head stiffly, she walked hurriedly and self-consciously to his work room. She stopped at the door, waiting for him to open it, and again she marveled at the beauty of the organized, beautifully appointed room. Bracken directed her to one of the desks and picked up a stack of paper.

"Start with these pages," he ordered. Then he went to the desk across from hers and sat down before the other typewriter.

Nervously, Summer settled into the chair and stared at the modern electric typewriter. Apprehensively, she looked across at Bracken and saw him watching her. She couldn't bear to have him see her discomfort, so she picked up a typed page and set it on the paper stand. As she skimmed it, her face clouded when she came to an especially racy passage, but she bravely inserted a sheet of paper and placed her fingers on the keys. With a sudden horror, she knew that she either had never learned to type or didn't remember how. Today of all days, she didn't want to appear incompetent, so she would have to manage somehow. She made her hands move, but all too soon it was obvious that she was not a typist.

She couldn't seem to make her fingers stretch to cover the keyboard; she was forced to resort to the hunt-and-peck method, probably the one she had always used if she had typed at all, and even at that, sometimes the typewriter seemed to want to run away with her. Aware of Bracken's gaze on her, she tried to fake her typing skills, but there was no help for her inadequacy. Not only did she seem to hit more incorrect keys than correct ones, she kept losing her place on the page she was working from. She resisted the urge to flee and continued to pretend to do the work. For about twenty minutes she banged away with disastrous results, obvious even to her untrained eyes. Then she heard heavy footsteps as Bracken approached her desk. She fought to slow her racing pulse and pounding heart, but his shadow fell relentlessly across her like an omen of doom.

"You can't type," he declared disdainfully. Opening the entryway to step behind the curved desk, he loomed above her as she bent over her work, trying vainly and foolishly to continue the sham.

Abruptly he bent down and yanked the paper from the machine. "Look at this mess! A monkey could do a better job!"

Summer had had all she could take of his attitude. She had been wrong last night, and she was sorry it had happened at all, but she couldn't change that. She could, however, do something about his behavior now.

Standing up and glaring at him with frosty blue eyes, she

retorted, "I'm sorry, Mr. Bohannon, that I don't live up to your expectations as a typist. However, I am not a monkey. If a monkey can do the work, perhaps you should get one, or do it yourself!"

Whirling away from him, she started to leave, but he caught her wrist and jerked her back to him. His eyes were stormy as they raked over her face. Suddenly he released her and leaned back against the desk.

"I didn't say you were a monkey," he growled. "And where do you think you're going? Put your shapely little rear back on this chair and try again. You may as well learn. You have to earn your room and board somehow."

Her eyes brilliant with anger, she shook her head defiantly. "I won't do your typing, and I wouldn't stay here in your house if there were anywhere else in the world I could go."

"Won't Desmond take you back?" he questioned savagely.

For the briefest of seconds Summer thought she would cry at the mention of the unknown Desmond, but she bit down on her lower lip and clenched her fists angrily. "I'm sure he would if I knew where to find him," she replied hotly.

"Well, then, I'll have to find him for you," Bracken snapped. "Never let it be said that I kept a woman from the man she wanted."

"I don't want—" Summer clamped her lips down on the words she had almost said to him. What an utter fool she was! After the way he had treated her, she had almost told him that he was the man she really wanted. How could she be so stupid?

"You don't want what?" he demanded, glaring coldly at her. "If you remember who this man is, by heaven you'd better tell me. You certainly came up with his name in the nick of time last night, didn't you?"

Before she had time to control her anger, Summer drew back a hand to slap his handsome face, but Bracken thwarted the blow.

"Don't throw a tantrum with me! I won't put up with it! I don't know how much Desmond stood for, but I'll tell you right now that I won't tolerate your little games. Tell me. Do you remember who this Desmond is?"

Summer tried futilely to picture Desmond, and the hopelessness of her position overwhelmed her. Dejectedly, she shook her head. She would give anything to be able to say she did know. She didn't know who Desmond was, and she didn't know who *she* was. And she didn't know where to go to escape Bracken and the attraction he held for her. She would have to endure his wrath until she had another place to live. It was a depressing situation no matter how you looked at it. And she had gone and complicated matters by falling in love with this unpredictable, cruel man. She didn't want him to turn her out, and yet she had no right to love him. She didn't know what ties she had to Desmond, but she knew Bracken couldn't be true to a woman.

Drawing a deep breath, Summer ignored her wounded pride and forced the apologetic words through tight lips. "I'll do the typing, and I *can* do it if you'll just show me where to put my fingers and give me a chance to practice."

For a moment Bracken's shuttered expression was unreadable. Then he grudgingly indicated the chair. Summer sat back down and bent her head in resignation. When Bracken leaned over her shoulder, she felt her blood race at the warmth of his body so near hers. Taking her hands in his, he placed them correctly on the keys and showed her how to stretch her fingers to reach the rows above and below the center line. Summer didn't breathe easily until he had straightened up.

"Practice as much as you want," he said curtly. "The

manuscript has to be perfect. I take pride in my work, and if you can't do it right, I'll do it myself."

"I'll do it right," she promised, each word full of brittle bitterness. By heavens, she would do it right, or she would die trying. Refusing to look at him again, she turned back to her task. It wasn't as difficult as she had thought once she had her fingers in the right position and she had put the paper stand nearer the typewriter so she could see more clearly. Soon she was doing a reasonably acceptable job and picking up a bit of speed. She kept at it doggedly until she was startled by a knock on the door.

"Lunch," Rose called out in the hard voice that hid her good nature.

Summer leaned back in her chair and stretched her muscles. She hadn't realized how cramped they were becoming with the unfamiliar task.

Bracken let Rose in, and when Summer saw the tempting club sandwiches piled on the plate, she began to feel hungry.

"What do you want to drink?" Rose asked, looking at Summer.

"Do you have any cola? I love it." As soon as she had said it, she blinked at the revelation. She had had no idea that she liked soda. She certainly hadn't had any desire for it in the past two days, but something about the sandwiches reminded her of how much she enjoyed it.

Rose nodded. "You're in luck. Harry drinks it, so I keep a supply on hand. I'll be right back." After setting the tray on the end of Bracken's desk, Rose turned toward the door.

"I'll get it," Summer insisted. "I don't want you to have to come all the way back up here just for me."

Rose waved her comment aside. "Nonsense. I get paid for doing it. You pull up your chair and have a sandwich."

Summer smiled at the woman, and she was surprised

when Bracken took a comfortable chair from its place by the window and set it across the desk from his own.

"I don't know about you," he said, "but I'm starving. I guess it's all the fighting we do."

Summer looked up at him warily, but when she saw his slight smile, she relaxed a little. She desperately wanted to apologize for her behavior the previous night, but she didn't dare bring the subject up. What could she possibly say in her defense?

In a few minutes Rose returned with Summer's soda, and Summer and Bracken settled down to their lunch and some surprisingly pleasant conversation.

"How long have you lived here?" Summer asked, curious about the area and wanting to make harmless small talk.

"I was born not far from here. My parents were rugged individualists. They settled in Big Sur before most people considered it suitable, much less desirable. For a long time we didn't have electricity, not that we couldn't afford it, but my father wanted things kept as close to the natural as possible. I've never forgotten some of the things he taught me about living with the land and nature." He smiled. "But I'm afraid I like comfort too much to do without the finer things in life. I think money is to be spent and, for me, a lot of pleasure is in modern conveniences. I've tried for a compromise here at Isolation—the primitive outside the house and a reasonable use of technology inside."

Summer returned his smile. He had achieved the compromise very well. "How many people live in the area now?"

"Less than a thousand. Most of them value their privacy. It's generally one of the reasons they move here, aside from the beauty of the area, of course. We do have get-togethers, though. A fund-raising event is coming up next week. A cookout. It should be fun."

"It sounds like it," Summer agreed, a little disappointed

that he hadn't mentioned taking her. "I could learn to love this area myself. It's magnificent. Dad and I lived in . . . in . . ." This was it! she thought incredulously. She almost had it. Where had she and her father lived? Her brows met in a line of irritation, and she struck her fist on the edge of the desk. "I forget where," she confessed miserably.

"When?"

"If I don't know where, I don't know when," she muttered.

"I was just trying some strategy of my own," he said, looking at her thoughtfully. "I think you're beginning to remember some things. It's a good sign. Don't push it, though. It will all work out."

Summer sighed in exasperation. "It's so nerve-racking. If I had any money I would pay a therapist to help me remember. I don't know why it's taking so long for my memory to return."

Bracken laced his long, lean fingers together and stretched them before him. "I don't think you need to see a therapist yet. Give it a little time. If things don't go well, we'll see about it later." He studied her face intently, but he said nothing else as he picked up another sandwich and bit into it.

When lunch was finished, they went back to work. This time Summer did much better, though her progress was painfully slow. She was fascinated with the story, but suddenly she looked up at Bracken as he worked across the room from her.

"You spelled *primavera* wrong," she said. "It's m-a-v, not m-i-v."

Bracken looked vaguely surprised. "How do you know how to spell in Spanish?"

She shrugged. "I don't know how I know, but I do. Look it up if you don't believe me. You spelled it wrong."

Bracken smiled and shook his head. "I would never

doubt anyone so adamant; I'm sure you're right. I'm just curious about your knowledge of the language. Of course, you could have studied it in school, but your accent sounds pretty good."

"Yes, I know," she said self-consciously. "I've been told that before." Suddenly she blushed. Why could she remember such trivial things and not who she was or where she was going or if she was married or where she lived? She gave a troubled shake of her head. "Well, I'll correct it on the copy."

"Fine," he agreed. *"Como te llama?"*

"No se," she replied, laughing lightly. "It's a good question, but I don't know what my name is."

"No," he said, "but you do speak Spanish. That's interesting, though not unusual in this neck of the woods." Looking back down at his typewriter, he resumed working.

Summer went back to her typing, but she couldn't keep her mind on it. Where had she learned to speak Spanish? Regardless of how hard she struggled to find answers, she drew the same old blank until her head hurt from trying to connect the bits and pieces that surfaced to tease and torment her. She kept at her chore, typing several more pages until Bracken stood up and stretched.

Surreptitiously, Summer watched him. He was disturbingly manly, and she shivered as she thought of that rugged body lying beside hers last night. She mustn't think such things, she chided herself. When he spoke to her, she started.

"How about dinner? I know a marvelous restaurant not far from here. It's world-renowned for its atmosphere and excellent food. The sun will be setting soon, and the restaurant patio has a great view of the ocean and the mountains along the coast."

"I'm convinced," Summer said, trying not to let her excitement show. "I'd love to go."

"Good. Get dressed and I'll meet you downstairs in half an hour. I'll have to tell Rose not to cook dinner for us."

Summer nodded nonchalantly, but for the life of her she couldn't control the dancing in her stomach. The thought of an evening with Bracken in such an atmosphere conjured up all kinds of romantic thoughts. And he was being very nice to her all of a sudden. She had to take herself sharply in hand to suppress her wild imaginings. After all, she couldn't bear a repeat of what had happened last evening. If only she knew her past. Something, anything, to tell her if she had known a man intimately before. Why was she behaving so brazenly with Bracken? Was it because she was in love with him? Or did she make a practice of such behavior?

She shuddered at the very thought. Yet she did keep remembering something about being a party girl. Was she married to the blond man named Desmond? Had she cheated on him, as Bracken seemed to think? Shaking her head, she stood up and strolled down the hall to her room. She seemed to be drawn to the wedding band, which she had put in a bureau drawer. Picking it up, she held it in her open palm. It was sized for a big man, so why did she have it in her possession? Had her husband thrown it at her in a fit of pique over something she had done?

Tears came to her eyes. She wanted desperately not to have a man in her past. She wanted to belong totally to Bracken Bohannon, and that might never be possible. Even if she had been married and could divorce her husband, she knew that Bracken could never be hers. He thought the worst possible things about her as it was, and after hearing that his wife had had a lover, Summer knew that Bracken would never let her attraction to him grow into anything more than an affair. She closed her eyes on the bitter thoughts and stood quietly for a moment, holding the ring. Then she tossed it back in the drawer and closed it. She couldn't change a thing by worrying about it, but she would give anything if she could remember.

Determinedly, she walked to her closet and pulled out the flowered caftan. Then she showered and slipped into it. The soft, flowing lines made her look very delicate and feminine. After slipping into a new pair of sandals, she traced her lips with a rose lip gloss and started down to meet Bracken.

Her glance skimmed quickly over him where he sat relaxing against the couch pillows. She was unable to avoid noticing the rigidly controlled waves of his rich chestnut hair, the cool gray eyes, the strong jaw, the width of his chest, which seemed ever broader in the pale gold sweater. The tobacco brown of his slacks emphasized his long legs. Summer's glance met his as he stood up.

"Good. You're ready."

She nodded, feeling slightly breathless as he approached her. He was obviously making an attempt to be nice to her, and she felt foolishly giddy with anticipation of the evening ahead. Lightly touching her elbow, Bracken guided her to the door, and she had to fight to quell the excitement she felt at his touch.

On the way to dinner, Summer could think of nothing to say. She stared at the passing scenery, content just to be near Bracken. When they reached the restaurant, she saw immediately that it was all that Bracken had claimed. Perched on the side of a hill, it afforded a stunning view of the white-capped waves of the ocean below and the staggered mountains up the coast.

"It really is beautiful," she breathed.

"Ah, I'm glad you approve," Bracken said warmly, directing her to a patio chair where she could look out over the canyons and ocean.

Summer looked up into his face and smiled happily at him.

"What can I get you to drink?" he asked.

"What are you drinking?" She couldn't seem to remember the names of drinks.

"A mai-tai. They're strong, but good. Do you want to try one?"

"Yes, please." Summer turned in her chair, watching as Bracken disappeared into the bar. Her imagination began to run wild. She actually began to think that she and Bracken Bohannon might have a future together. He was attracted to her, although she conceded that it might be only physical at this time. But maybe things could be different once they found out about her past. She found herself praying, *Please God, don't let me be married.* She was still staring at the door when Bracken came out with two drinks in his hands, smiling at her.

"Don't watch the door," he teased. "I brought you here to show you the fabulous sunset. Have you ever seen such an inspiring sight?" he asked, looking out at the oranges and reds of the evening sky as the sun hung over the dark blue expanse of the ocean.

Reluctantly, Summer looked away from Bracken to stare out at the view, and she had to agree that it was truly beautiful. In silence, they watched the sun slip lower and lower until only a sliver of orange showed above the sea. Summer sipped her drink, feeling a contentment she hadn't experienced since the accident. She felt that she could stay in that spot with Bracken by her side forever.

When darkness draped the hills, Summer shivered a little at the drop in temperature.

"Cold?" Bracken murmured. "Do you want to go in for dinner now?"

"Oh, not yet," she said quickly. "Let's stay out here a little longer."

"All right." Summer sucked in her breath when he

wrapped his arm around her shoulders and hugged her to him. "Is that better?"

Her mouth was suddenly dry, and her heart was pounding wildly at his nearness. All she could do was nod, and she doubted if he saw the motion in the descending darkness.

"Are you very concerned about the future, Summer?" he asked seriously. "You know that you can stay at Isolation until you're able to work something out for yourself. I'm sure some answers will come from somewhere. Ellen Story will return to her apartment sooner or later, even if your memory proves elusive for a while longer."

Summer was comforted by his thoughtful reassurances, but following that short moment of happiness, she felt a little forlorn at the idea of Ellen Story returning to solve the mystery. She wanted to find her own way, and she wanted to stay with Bracken as long as she could. If Ellen turned up with the pieces to the puzzle, would Summer be able to face them without knowing herself?

"Summer, did you hear me?"

"Yes. Yes, I did, and I appreciate your willingness to let me stay, Bracken. It's very kind of you, since I don't mean anything to you. I'm just a stranger who ran into your car in the fog."

Summer's face flamed when Bracken made no reply, and she was glad he couldn't see it in the darkness. She had been hoping he would tell her he wanted her to stay. She had been unconsciously seeking some kind of commitment from him.

"Are you ready to eat now?" he asked, and Summer felt a twinge of regret that they were going in.

"Yes," she said quietly, standing up as Bracken withdrew the warmth of his arm.

Taking her hand in his, he led the way to the restaurant.

Just as he opened the door for them to enter, Summer heard a female voice call out from behind them.

"Bracken! Bracken!"

Reluctantly, Summer paused and turned as Darlene Draper rushed up to them. Bracken held the door open for the other women to enter, and Summer tried to suppress the unreasonable dislike she felt for Darlene.

"Good evening, cousin," Darlene said tauntingly when they were inside. "I see you're still with us." Turning to Bracken, she linked her arm in his. "I'm so glad I caught up with you before you were seated, darling. May I join you for dinner?"

Summer stared at the woman as bitter resentment and jealousy rose in her, two emotions she had no right to feel. Bracken certainly didn't belong to her. Summer's glance traveled down Darlene's tall frame. Dressed in a long, clinging orange gown, her brown hair piled provocatively on her head in a mass of saucy curls, the woman was smiling sweetly at Bracken.

"Yes, of course," Bracken replied. "You don't mind, do you, Summer?" he asked, facing her.

What could she say? That she minded with all her heart? That she had wanted the evening to be a special one for just the two of them?

"No, of course not," she murmured, unable to meet his gaze. Her eyes met Darlene's, and she was sure the woman smiled smugly at her.

Summer trailed solemnly along behind Darlene as the woman chatted incessantly to Bracken while they were being escorted to a table.

"This is wonderful," Darlene said with a throaty laugh when she sat down and pulled Bracken into the chair beside her. "It gives me an excuse to sit near you, not that I need one, but we're usually across the table from each other."

As Summer seated herself across from them, she tried not to look at the cozy picture they made. She had to pretend that she wasn't being consumed with a totally unreasonable jealousy. For all she knew she had a husband somewhere. What was she doing hating this woman for being Bracken's lover?

Chapter Six

Summer was sitting by a window, and for several seconds she stared out at the silhouetted dark. She sighed and tried to block out Darlene's purring voice. Bracken ordered another drink for each of them, and in spite of herself, Summer began to relax as she sipped the potent mai-tai.

When their meal arrived, Summer found hers delicious, and she concentrated on it while Darlene carried on a monologue about her job. She was a reporter and worked in Monterey, but she was going to do a piece for a big newspaper about the upcoming Big Sur fundraiser.

Summer soon became preoccupied with her own thoughts, but she made appropriate replies whenever she was spoken to, usually by Bracken. She pretended to give her attention to her meal, and the time somehow passed.

After Summer had eaten the last bite of her steak, she leaned back and watched Bracken speculatively while he listened intently to Darlene. Her eyes strayed to the window again. She could learn to love this area, she mused reflectively, as much as she loved Bracken Bohannon. But as if her situation weren't complicated enough already, there was the matter of Darlene, the other woman.

Just as she thought the words, something flickered in Summer's mind. She fought desperately to cling to the idea, and she was partially successful. She envisioned Desmond again, and another woman—a dark, exotic woman. She was laughing at Summer, taunting her, and Desmond was—no! She had lost it. Just when she was on to something concrete. What had it been? Why had the woman been laughing at her? Why had she been with Desmond? It was so frustrating to get so near and then end up with disjointed and disappointing fragments.

"Summer!"

Blinking, Summer looked up into Bracken's eyes as he leaned toward her.

"I've been trying to break through your concentration. We're going to have an after-dinner drink. Will you join us?"

"Yes," she agreed quickly, embarrassed by her momentary retreat into her fragmented thoughts. "I'm sorry. I was thinking."

"Obviously. May I suggest an Irish coffee? It's coffee with sugar, whipped cream, and whiskey."

"Fine."

Summer fought not to retreat into her thoughts, and when the Irish coffee arrived, she found that it was delicious. She felt quite relaxed by the time Darlene stood up and asked Bracken to escort her to the ladies' lounge.

Bracken excused himself and Summer watched as the two of them disappeared. It was only seconds later that two young men sat down at the table beside hers. The one nearest her smiled, and Summer innocently smiled back.

When the hostess handed the man the menu, he leaned close to Summer and asked, "What do you suggest? This is our first time in this restaurant. We're from Nevada."

Summer smiled again. "It's my first time, too, and I don't know where I'm from."

Apparently thinking she was making a joke, the man laughed delightedly and repeated her comment for his companion, who then joined in the laughter. Bracken chose just that moment to return and found the three of them laughing together. He looked coldly at Summer, and his stare had the effect of a splash of cold water on all three of them. Staring deliberately at their menus, the two men left Summer to face Bracken's dissatisfaction alone.

"A man can't be out of your sight for twenty seconds before you start to hunt for another one, can he?" Bracken asked in a low growl, sitting down.

"I didn't start to hunt for another one," Summer retorted defensively.

Bracken held up a warning hand. "Please, spare me. We'll discuss it some other time."

"There's nothing to discuss—"

As Darlene returned to the table, Bracken stood up, effectively silencing Summer's protests. "Ready?" he asked, including both women in the question.

Summer had no alternative but to stand up and follow the two of them out. Being careful not to give the two men beside her so much as a glance, she walked stiffly from the restaurant.

When they reached Bracken's car, Summer saw that Darlene had parked right beside it. Bracken unlocked Darlene's car door, but as he stepped back for her to enter, she suddenly pulled his head toward hers and kissed him passionately.

Summer felt really angry now. Not only was she feeling jealous, but she considered the bold display to be in poor taste, since she was waiting for Bracken to unlock her car door. Stalking to the passenger side of his car, she waited in silent fury for him to leave Darlene.

On the return drive to Isolation both of them were silent; the tension in the air fairly crackled. Summer wanted nothing more than to leave his company, and she seethed with anger while the car wound its way back to the house. As soon as Bracken parked, Summer jerked open her door and marched away. As on that earlier occasion, the front door was locked. This time she pushed impatiently at the doorbell, refusing to wait for Bracken.

Rose, with Devil at her heels, answered and stood staring curiously at Summer, then at Bracken, who was coming up the walk.

Summer knew that her anger was unreasonable, but she couldn't help herself, and she stormed inside, past the housekeeper. She was in love with Bracken Bohannon, and she wasn't in the mood to be rational. She had anticipated a romantic evening with him. Instead, she had become the third wheel, which had dramatically emphasized what a fool she had been to succumb to his charms. She had actually begun to think he cared for her! What kind of idiot was she? Did she generally go around putting her heart in jeopardy when she had been warned about a man? If Marissa Bohannon had been subjected to Bracken's infidelity, what made Summer think he had any scruples along that line, much less any allegiance to her? Had he told Darlene to meet them at the restaurant? Had Summer's behavior the previous night so angered him that he had wanted to teach her a lesson?

"I had a terrible evening," she murmured to Rose. "Please excuse me."

Rose shook her head in confusion, but she remained silent as she turned back down the hall.

Summer had started up the steps when she heard the front door slam. Bracken charged into the house and up the stairs behind her. Summer hastened her steps, but it was no use. Bracken reached for her arm and dragged her back down to the living room.

"I told you not to throw your little tantrums with me," he said warningly, staring coldly down into her blazing blue eyes. "You're angry about Darlene, aren't you? That's why you flirted with those men, isn't it? I'm seeing more and more reasons why your husband turned you out."

"My husband didn't turn me out, if, indeed, I have one," she retorted sharply. "I was the one running away, not him. And you do flatter yourself to think I care what you do with Darlene."

"Do I?" he snapped. "Come on. Admit it. You were jealous of Darlene. You didn't want her to join us for dinner. You made it quite apparent. Well, she's an old friend, and I couldn't very well have refused."

"I am not jealous of your 'old friend,'" Summer cried. "I was embarrassed by your public display, that's all. I don't care what the two of you do in private, but don't make me watch!"

"You *are* jealous," he accused.

"Not in your lifetime."

"You are," he insisted, a wicked gleam appearing in his eyes. "Well, don't behave rashly. I can't abide such behavior, and I can see that you're prone to it."

"If you mean rash like your wife's behavior, Mr. Bohannon, have no fear on that score. I don't care how many mistresses you have. I just resent being treated shabbily by anyone. I'm not used to it, and I won't put up with it. The next time you invite me someplace, don't flaunt your paramour in my face!"

Even as she said the words, a painful memory surfaced in her mind. Had she been treated shabbily by the blond man? What was his name? She couldn't think of it in her agitation. Was that the reason she had been driving the rented car? Was she running away from heartache? Disappointment? Was there something between the blond man and the dark woman? Was he Summer's husband, and had *he* been the one who cheated?

Cruel fingers suddenly bit into the tender flesh on her upper arm. "I wasn't thinking of my wife's behavior, and her accident wasn't the result of me taking a mistress—at least, not any mistress you know about!" he growled.

Summer gasped as she stared up into his cruel eyes. His naked pain was devastatingly apparent, and she had never thought of Bracken as being vulnerable. Still, she refused to relent and comfort him.

"Then you do admit that there was a mistress and that you drove your wife away!"

"My wife was the same kind of tease you are," he told her. "She couldn't seem to leave other men alone. She was just like you; all a man had to do was touch her, and she gave in to him."

Summer blanched. "I don't fall into the arms of any man who pays attention to me! And the biggest mistake I've made so far was falling into yours!"

"Oh?" he snarled, and before she could turn away, he bent his head and kissed her cruelly. She tried to fight him, but she was no match for his towering strength, and soon she knew it was useless to struggle.

When it appeared that he thought she was submitting to his touch, his kiss turned less savage, and Summer felt a tremor go through her body. She did want him, it was true. She wanted him desperately, but she couldn't make herself believe that she was the kind of girl to give in to every man. She just couldn't believe it. And yet her actions seemed contradictory when she was near Bracken. Though she fought fiercely against the urge to wrap her arms around his broad back, she found herself doing just that. And to her shame, when he felt her arms around him, he released her abruptly.

"Need more proof?" he asked, his eyes gleaming triumphantly. Then he turned and strolled toward his study.

"Ohhh!" Summer cried, biting down on her bottom lip and struggling to hold back a flood of bitter, angry tears. He was horrible! He was a cruel, calculating demon! How could she be in love with him? She should hate him with every inch of her!

As she watched him disappear, Summer's shoulders suddenly slumped in weary defeat. She should hate him, but, of course, she didn't. She loved Bracken Bohannon, and her anger and disappointment couldn't alter that tragic fact a bit. On shaking legs, she climbed the stairs and went to her room, where she threw herself down on the bed.

She felt awful. She had to get out of Bracken's house. She was falling apart from the tension and the torture of her situation. She had to get away, but once again reason overshadowed desire. Where on earth would she go? If the police discovered anything, they would come to this house to inform her. How would she ever find out who she was if she left? She burst into bitter tears. Once again she was devastated by the knowledge that she had no past, and without it, a very uncertain future.

Sometime in the night Summer awakened with a jolt and stared around the room. She was sure she had dreamed that she was running away from the blond man, fleeing from his touch. A damp line of perspiration moistened her forehead, and she reached up to wipe it away. Then she breathed a sigh of relief. She wasn't with the blond man, and she wasn't running away. She was safe in Bracken's house.

She tried to make some sense of the dream, but again there were only bits and pieces available to her; she finally reasoned that it had resulted from her dispute with Bracken. She really didn't know anything about herself or the blond man. Maybe he was just a figment of her imagination.

Trembling in the blackness of the room, she stared up at the skylight and saw that there were no stars out, and even the crescent moon was vanishing behind gathering clouds. She shivered a little as she slid off the bed to undress. Needing to find something comforting, she reached for Bracken's tee shirt and slipped into it. For some reason it made her feel more secure. That was ridiculous, of course, but she was able to get back to sleep without much effort. And this time she slept until the morning dawned.

As was his habit, Devil whined at her door before seven o'clock. This morning she wanted his company, and she went to the door to let him in. To her chagrin, Bracken was strolling down the hall toward the dog. Spying Summer, his hard eyes skimmed over her disheveled form, lost in the big tee shirt. Her body responded to his bold scrutiny, and she attempted to shut the door, but Devil had already started in, and it was impossible. Summer had no recourse but to stand as far behind the door as she could until Bracken called the dog.

He did call, but today Devil had ideas of his own. This was his first invitation into Summer's room, and he was not to be denied. Ignoring his master's voice, he bounded toward Summer's bed, and with one clumsy jump, he had landed in the middle of it.

Brushing past her with a frigid look, Bracken approached the animal, grasped him by his collar and dragged him from the room. His eyes sweeping over her once again, he pulled the dog out and down the hall before he released him. Summer quickly closed the door before either of them could reenter. She was shaking like a leaf.

Forcing herself into the shower, she bathed quickly and then dressed in a simple brown dress she had selected when she and Bracken went shopping. She would have to go on with her day; she would have to pretend that there was nothing wrong between them. She would bite her tongue and go to his workroom to do the typing. It was the only way she had of earning her keep, and no matter how she disliked having to face him today, it couldn't be helped.

So intent was she on her task that she almost forgot to eat breakfast. She was already headed toward his office when she realized that she was hungry. Changing direction, she hurried down the stairs to the kitchen.

Bracken glanced at her as she sat down, but he said nothing. Rose came into the room, her features set as she asked Summer what she wanted for breakfast. A quick glance at Bracken's plate showed the remains of his usual bacon and eggs and Summer asked for the same. After Rose set a cup of coffee before Summer, she left the room. Bracken picked up his newspaper to read in silence.

Summer gazed at him for a moment, noticing that he was dressed in blue jeans and a blue shirt, a contrast to the sweaters and colored jeans he usually wore. Then she turned to her meal, eating it quickly. She wanted to be ready to go up to work when Bracken left the table. However, he surprised her when she was almost finished with her breakfast.

"I'll show you the grounds today," he said evenly.

"But why?"

"Why?" he repeated, staring at her with an unfathomable expression.

"I mean, aren't we going to work today?" she asked in a more normal tone. "Don't you write every day?"

"It's cloudy today. When the weather is like this, I enjoy riding," he said, as though it were the most logical explanation in the world. "It's good thinking weather," he added. "And the horses need exercise." He looked at her sharply. "You don't have to come if you don't want to."

She wanted to, of course, but she didn't want to sound too eager. "I don't mind," she said.

"Well, don't put yourself out any."

Summer sighed. Was this how love was? Was it always fighting and bickering and screaming and accusing? She reminded herself at once of how absurd her thoughts were. This man wasn't in love with her, and she had no right to be in love with him.

She looked up at him, trying to disguise her thoughts, and forced a tight little smile to her lips. "It's very thoughtful of you to invite me to ride with you, and I would like to very much."

This new strategy obviously caught him unprepared; it took him a minute to decide if she were being sincere. "Fine," he said at last. "Put on jeans and sturdy shoes and a jacket. It's a little cold out today."

"I'll only be a moment," she said, rising rapidly. She was so pleased at the prospect that she had to take herself in hand to keep from skipping out of the room. When she had shut her bedroom door, she swiftly changed into the outfit Bracken had suggested, appraising herself in the jeans and western shirt and finding the image pleasing. Grabbing a light jacket, she was on her way back downstairs in less than five minutes.

A glance from Bracken told her that he was satisfied with her clothes, and he stood up. Rose entered to hand him a canteen and a leather bag with a strap. Side by side, Bracken and Summer strolled out the front door and down the walk. She tried in vain to hide her pleasure at the outing. Looking down at her, Bracken saw her smile and returned it.

"Do you know if you ride?" he asked her, just a hint of teasing in his voice. "And don't say 'doesn't everybody.' "

Summer shrugged slightly. "No, I don't know, but I'm sure I can learn if I can't," she added, her stomach tensing at the idea that he might refuse to take her.

"Yes, I'm sure you can," he said agreeably, and Summer smiled again, indescribably happy that he wasn't angry with her today.

They walked past the vegetable garden, and for the first time Summer noticed that an area was fenced off for the horses. Harry had already rounded up the animals and was saddling one when they approached. A big brown stallion tossed his head and nickered softly when he saw Bracken.

"This is Charlie," Bracken said. "He looks formidable, but, like Devil, he's an old softy."

"I'll take your word for it," Summer said, eyeing an old mare and finding her much more to her liking.

Following her gaze, Bracken laughed. "Yes, you can ride Mabel," he said without being asked. "She really is a gentle old nag. I've had her for years. The other one," he gestured to a large young filly, which hung back from the other two, "is a bit wild. It seems that everyone who rides selects either Charlie or Mabel and Nancy is generally spurned."

Summer looked at Nancy. "Well, I agree with everyone else, and she's going to be spurned today, too," she declared with a light laugh. "She looks too spirited to suit me."

Swinging himself easily over the log fence, Bracken stroked Mabel's neck, and the old mare followed him through the gate and into the stable. He saddled her, then looped her reins over the fence post. Harry had saddled Charlie by the time Bracken saddled Mabel, and he wished them a good ride and ambled back toward the house, stopping for a minute to look at the vegetable garden.

Bracken looped Charlie's reins over the post and turned to Summer. "Well, let's take a chance. Climb aboard."

Summer's only moment of hesitation occurred when Bracken handed her the reins. Approaching the animal, she realized that she did, indeed, know how to ride; grasping the reins, she hopped high enough to insert her left foot in the stirrup. Standing straight up in the left stirrup, it was an easy matter to swing her right leg over the horse's rump and down into the right stirrup.

Summer felt just a little smug at finding something besides cooking that she could do with no difficulty, and she smiled triumphantly at Bracken.

He saluted her with a wave and a big grin before mounting Charlie and turning the horse away from the stable and into the thick stands of trees and dense vegetation. Feeling slightly exhilarated as they broke into a canter, Summer followed behind the strong stallion and his towering rider. For some time they rode single file along a trail that both horses were apparently familiar with.

Summer raised brilliant eyes to the pine trees around them and inhaled deeply, glorying in the fresh scent and noting the cushioned feel of the brown pine needles beneath the horse's hooves. Scrub oaks, dense growth, and brambles were nearly too thick to pass through in some spots, and they slowed to a walk. Bracken turned around occasionally to look at Summer, and once he called over his shoulder to ask if she was making out all right.

"Fine," she called out gaily. In fact, she couldn't remember when she had felt better. Despite the gray clouds and the mist that hung over the forest, Summer found it to be beautiful and fascinating. The calm and peaceful woods were actually alive with the activity of their inhabitants. Finches and blue jays flew among the trees, and Summer was sure she saw quail on the ground. She listened to the cheerful notes of the finches' song, and she heard the noisy fussing of the jays. Woodrats dropped their seeds and scurried for cover when the horses approached, and a single lizard darted boldly across their path. When the horses worked their way down a hillside,

Summer could see a blue stream flowing lazily along the bottom of the canyon.

Bracken slowed down and waited for Summer to ride alongside him on the narrow path. "Look there in the thicket," he whispered, indicating some dense bushes.

Turning curious eyes in the direction where he pointed, Summer gasped as she saw a small blacktail deer lying down, partially hidden in the undergrowth, her eyes wide and frightened, her muscles tensed for flight. Bracken and Summer watched for only a moment, unwilling to upset the deer further, then continued down the trail, leaving the animal to its hideaway.

"She was gorgeous," Summer said a moment later. "Are there many deer here?"

"Yes. They're increasing all the time, so there's little danger of them becoming extinct."

"What other animals live here?" she asked.

"A lot of raccoons, but don't expect to see any. They're nocturnal, so they won't be out until the sun goes down. There are coyotes here and skunks. We have wild pigs, too, but they tend to avoid people unless a sow feels that her piglets are threatened and is put in the position of defending them. They're generally shy, but of course they can be very dangerous. A boar can weigh as much as six hundred pounds and get to be five feet long. I wouldn't tangle with one, I'll tell you."

"I should hope not," Summer breathed, growing apprehensive at the very thought. "Are you sure we won't meet one today?" The idea was frightening, even with Bracken along.

He laughed softly. "They're rarely seen in the daylight, although the first rain of a season may bring them out to dig for roots." He watched her wide-eyed expression. "Don't worry. I won't let a hair on your head be harmed." His eyes twinkled. "You've already done enough damage to it."

Automatically, Summer reached up to tug at the short strands of her hair. "It doesn't look bad, Bracken," she insisted.

He laughed deeply, then urged his horse forward. Throwing her a glance over his shoulder, he conceded, "No, it doesn't. I rather like it now that I'm used to it, but I have so much fun teasing you."

"Oh!" she cried, but he was prodding Charlie into a gallop, and Summer had to nudge Mabel firmly with her thighs to get the old mare to pick up her pace. The horse seemed heedless of Summer's coaxing, and she watched, a little alarmed, as Bracken outdistanced her. Her anxiety was unwarranted, for he stopped up ahead of her and waited for her to catch up.

When she came out into the clearing, she saw that they had reached the wide stream. It was quite romantic with its blue water gurgling over smooth pebbles and rocks, its sandy banks, and lush, low-hanging trees.

Bracken swung down from his horse with a minimum of motion, hooking Charlie's reins to a branch. Bracken came to Summer and reached up for her; she smiled down into his eyes as he lifted her from her horse. When he stood her on her feet, his hands remained firmly about her waist. Shimmering blue eyes stared expectantly into deep gray ones as Summer held her breath in anticipation of his kiss. Instead of fulfilling her expectations, Bracken grinned and suddenly gave her a slap on her rear.

Summer winced visibly. She hadn't realized until she was on the ground that she was unaccustomed to the bouncing motion of the horse. She knew how to ride, but it must have been some time since she had done so.

"Uh oh," Bracken murmured. "I think you're going to have some sore muscles from this."

Summer blushed, aware that the playful slap that had been intended to break the tension between them had only embarrassed them both. "I think you might be right," she admitted.

A slight grin returned to his lips. "Later today we'll take a swim to loosen up those muscles, and we'll sit in the sauna for a while. That will get you back in shape in no time. You did buy a swimsuit, didn't you?"

Summer nodded, thinking how carefully she had selected the suit in anticipation of just such an occasion.

"Darn!" Bracken teased, snapping his fingers in pretended irritation. "And I was going to suggest that we swim in the nude."

Summer blushed again and looked away. She had already seen Bracken naked once, and that memory seared across her mind. Once had been enough.

"Well," he said, turning away to reclaim his rested horse, "let's go downstream until we find ourselves a spot to rest."

He picked up Charlie's reins, and Summer gathered Mabel's in hand. Together, the horses trailing slowly behind, she and Bracken strolled along the sandy banks of the stream, occasionally ducking to avoid a tree or sidestepping a bushy shrub. When they reached a small clearing in the thick trees, Bracken asked, "How about this? Does it suit you?"

"Definitely," Summer agreed, looking about at the thick carpet of leaves covering the ground. Ancient, stately redwoods formed a canopy over the little spot, and lush ferns grew in profusion.

Bracken looped Charlie's reins lightly around a bush and took a red blanket from behind the saddle. Summer dismounted and followed Bracken's example, leaving her horse where she could drink from the stream, then helped Bracken spread the blanket on the ground. A squirrel watched them with curious eyes for a couple of minutes before vanishing into a hole in a nearby tree. He reappeared higher up and noisily chastised them for their intrusion. Bracken and Summer laughed at the little animal as Summer dropped down on the blanket and stretched out.

"Are we still on your land?" she asked, watching as Bracken took the leather sack from the saddle horn and sat down on the blanket beside her.

"Yes. Forty acres is a good-sized piece of land," he told her.

"Where does the stream go?"

"It flows into the ocean."

"Oh." She picked up a dead leaf and turned it over in her slender hand.

Bracken opened up the sack and produced cheese, crackers, a flask of wine, and two tin mugs. "Lunch," he declared with a grin, and Summer laughed delightedly.

"How wonderful," she cried. "A picnic!"

Bracken handed her a thick slice of cheddar cheese and two large crackers, then poured her a mug of wine. She was thrilled that he had thought of bringing food along, and she ate with enthusiasm, enjoying his company and her surroundings. The two of them finished the snack and drank the contents of the wine flask, then Bracken put the containers back in the sack.

"Are your muscles beginning to ache?" he asked, studying her face.

She moved her head in a circle. "My neck is a little stiff," she said with a gentle laugh. She hadn't given any thought to her muscles. "I must be a lady strictly used to the easy life."

Bracken slid over next to her and began to massage her slender neck with long, skilled fingers. Summer felt her breath catch in her throat. She could hardly bear to sit so near him and not be in his arms. She moaned softly as his hands worked their way down her back. She twisted her head to look at him, and he eased her down on the blanket.

"Summer, my sweet torment," he murmured, leaning over her. His lips descended to hers, and Summer molded her body to his as he stretched out over her. She gloried in the feel of him pressed so fiercely against her. His kiss deepened, and she wrapped her arms around his broad back, tracing the hard muscles with her hands. She felt the embers of passion smolder inside her as he caressed her willing flesh. His kiss grew reckless and bold, and her senses were inflamed as every fiber in her responded to his caress. She was left gasping when he lifted his mouth from hers and pulled back a little to stare into her brilliant, shining blue eyes. Her lips remained moist and softly parted. His mouth again descended to coax a fiery kiss from them.

Summer met his ardor with a flaming desire of her own, heedless of the consequences or the cost to her heart. Bracken's lips left hers to scorch the tender skin of her throat, and she breathed raggedly as he undid the buttons of the western shirt to claim her rapidly rising and falling breasts. Her fingers gripped his hair tightly as he teased her soft flesh with the tip of his tongue.

Suddenly he gathered her hungrily to him, murmuring in a strangled voice, "God knows I want you." He buried his face in the curve of her shoulder, and Summer felt the heavy thudding of her heart. Then, before she could catch her breath, he shoved her from him. "Damn you and damn Desmond, whoever the two of you are."

He sat up and thrust his hands through the rich waves of his hair. He cleared his throat before he spoke again, his casual tone concealing the hostility he was feeling. "I'm thirsty. Do you want a drink of water?"

Summer's throat was too constricted to allow her to speak. She swallowed hard once, then twice, and still she could only shake her head as she averted her eyes. Bracken seemed to delight in torturing her, taking her to the fringes of ecstasy, then pulling back and leaving her to teeter on the cliff alone.

He stood up, walked over to the horses, lifted the canteen from his saddle horn and took a long drink of water, keeping his back to Summer. It was several moments before he returned to the blanket and sat down.

Summer inhaled deeply; then, determined to find some shreds of her dignity and make the most of the lovely area, she forced her lips into a brittle smile. She couldn't help loving Bracken, but she could help letting him know it.

Stretching out on the blanket, Bracken cradled his head in his hands and closed his eyes with a deep sigh. Summer stretched out on her side and watched him for several minutes until his breathing became deep and even. With a weary sigh of her own, she lay down beside him and closed her eyes. The blond man's face unexpectedly swam before her eyes, and she found herself sharing Bracken's sentiments about the unknown Desmond. Whoever he was, she was finding it regrettably easy to hate him.

Chapter Seven

Summer awakened with a jolt and looked up into Bracken's brooding gray eyes. He was propped up on one elbow, watching her.

"Oh," she murmured, running a hand over her face and blinking uncomfortably as she suddenly remembered the strained scene that had taken place between them before they had slept. Her gaze fell away from his, and she felt a flush of embarrassment as she remembered the way she had gone into his arms so willingly. "I was sound asleep," she said confusedly.

"Yes, you were. We both were," Bracken said curtly. "It's after four o'clock. Are you ready to go back to the house?"

Summer glanced at him as he stood up and stretched. Even though his features were set in a hard line, she couldn't help but admire his good looks. She stood up slowly and drew a deep breath. The nap there in the quiet woods beside Bracken had been the most refreshing sleep she had enjoyed in days. "I'm ready," she agreed, stepping off the blanket. She reached down and picked up an end to help Bracken fold it. "I feel quite refreshed. I slept very well, in spite of—" She quickly closed her mouth. She had almost said in spite of being so upset.

Bracken's eyes swept over her, and the hard lines of his mouth gradually softened into a gentle smile. "I'm glad to know you enjoyed sleeping with me."

She smiled at the irony behind his words and thought ruefully that he was the one who had drawn the stops on their lovemaking. She had lost her resolve the moment he held her in his arms, and she was sure that she would have yielded completely to his fiery caresses if he had continued.

Dinner was ready by the time Bracken and Summer had worked their way back to the house. Neither of them felt especially hungry, but Rose had already set the table and had dinner ready to serve. She and Harry had eaten and were going into Monterey to visit with an old crony of Harry's. Bracken and Summer washed up for dinner, then settled down in the dining room while Rose rushed about getting the food on the table.

Summer smiled ruefully when she saw that Rose had prepared a special meal. The table looked lovely, and as Summer looked across at Bracken, she wished she could relax.

"Will there be anything else?" Rose asked, putting the remaining dishes on the table. "There's hot apple pie on the kitchen counter."

"Everything's fine, Rose. Thank you," Bracken said. "You and Harry go ahead ahead with your plans. We can manage from here."

Rose nodded. "Very well, Mr. Bohannon. Now, we'll be late tonight getting home."

"That's fine, Rose. Enjoy the evening."

"Same to you, sir." She turned and strode briskly from the room.

"Have you been able to remember where you learned to speak Spanish?" Bracken asked Summer abruptly.

Summer hadn't given it much thought, what with all the other things going on in her head. "No, I haven't."

Bracken looked thoughtfully at her before he poured dressing on his salad. "I wonder if you've spent any time in Mexico. It's entirely possible, with Mexico being our nearest neighbor. Are you familiar with Acapulco? Mexico City? Guadalajara? Monterrey?"

A distant memory stirred when Bracken rolled the r's in Monterrey. Summer frowned, searching for a missing piece to the puzzle.

Bracken studied her for a moment, then said, "Summer? Did I trigger something?"

She looked into his eyes and sighed wearily as she shook her head.

"Are you sure?" he pressed. "What were you thinking just then?"

She spread her hands helplessly. "It was nothing. Nothing. When you rolled the r's in Monterrey, I thought I connected it with something, but I'm grasping at straws in the wind. We've been in Monterey recently, and I guess that's why it sounded familiar to me." She laughed lightly. "See, I was hoping."

"That's all right," he said. "Leave all avenues of communication open. The trick is to penetrate the block to the past, even with a tiny hole, and let the facts seep in where they may. Don't get discouraged. There'll be a breakthrough."

She nodded, but she knew that they were both disappointed. She had been silly to even say anything. Of course Monterey sounded familiar; she had been there three times recently. She picked up her fork and took a bite of her salad, but her thoughts were complex and disturbing.

"I'm on the last chapter of *Dance with Danger,*" Bracken said, changing the subject. "Tomorrow we'll put in a full day's work."

"I've only read ten pages," Summer said. "Can I take it to bed with me tonight? I could type a little faster if I didn't become so engrossed in the story. Does Danielle get out of the well?"

Bracken chuckled. "I don't know yet, but I suppose she'll have to, wicked woman that she is." His eyes twinkled as he smiled at her. "Do you really think you could type any faster, regardless of the reason? What's your speed, about twenty words a minute?"

Her eyes met his, and she tried to contain the hurt she felt. Then she realized that he was teasing. "Ten," she said, trying to get into the spirit of the game, but she was sorry she couldn't type well enough to be of any real assistance to him and that made laughing about it difficult. What *could* she do? she wondered self-pityingly. She could cook and she could ride a horse, neither asset very beneficial to a writer. What had she done in the past? She hadn't been a secretary, that was for sure, but what had she done? Did she work? Go to school? Keep house? She struck the last thought from her mind. If she kept house, she must have a husband, and she wanted desperately to believe that she had never known love in any man's arms but Bracken's. When he spoke her name, she looked up guiltily.

"I beg your pardon," she murmured, red-faced.

"I said please pass the sour cream."

She reached for the dish so quickly that she almost knocked it over. "I'm sorry," she said, turning her whole attention to the meal. The food really was delicious, and she began to eat with a little more interest.

They lingered over dinner, and the coffee and pie that followed, until almost seven o'clock. They talked more about Bracken's latest book, and Summer asked to see some of the others he had written. Pleased that she was interested, Bracken led the way to the library.

Summer was astonished at the prodigious amount of work he had turned out, and she was enthralled by the rows of books. "But you've written so many!" she exclaimed, running her hands along the books. "Why, there must be twenty here."

"Twenty-four," he said dryly, and Summer turned to stare at him, surprised at his tone of voice. His face was etched with what she could only describe as bitter regret.

"Writing is my life. Anyone who hopes to be the center of attention with me must realize that they can never, never come first. If I don't write, I don't exist." He looked away from her to stare at the books with a hard expression in his eyes. "It's a cold reality for a woman to face," he said harshly. "Marissa couldn't cope with it." He looked back at Summer, and she held her breath in anticipation of his next statement, wondering painfully if it were the mistress or the writing that Marissa hadn't been able to cope with. "Could you take second place to a man's career, Summer?"

It seemed that the tension grew until it filled the room while Summer contemplated her answer. She wanted to cry out that she would take any place just to be with him, but that wasn't the question he had asked her, and she had too much pride to throw herself at him again. She phrased her reply carefully and said as indifferently as she could, "I don't know. I think it would depend on the man and how much I loved him."

His eyes were cold as they flicked over her figure and returned to her face. "You couldn't, any more than Marissa could," he said bluntly. Then he bent and pulled several books from the shelf.

"This is my first one. I'm sure you'll see my inexperience in it, but I had a story to tell and that carried the book." He handed it to her and indicated another one. "This is the one I wrote the year I was twenty-one and filled with the ego of manhood, but it's not a bad work. This one," he said, handing her another, "is my last one. An author leaves a little something of himself in all of his books, and this one smacks of heartache and disappointment, but the story is driving and compelling and it's considered to be my best book to date." He straightened and laughed a little. "My God, I sound like a pompous fool. I don't really take myself that seriously, but if I don't care, who else will? Please don't feel obligated to read them."

"I want to read them," she assured him. "I'd like to read them all." Especially the last one, she wanted to add, but of course she didn't want him to know that she wanted to see how he had reacted to the death of the woman he had married. That, of course, was the reason the last book was filled with heartache and disappointment. Bracken had been shattered over Marissa's death when he wrote it. As Summer thought about it, she almost changed her mind. She didn't want to know how much Bracken had cared for his dead wife. Resisting an urge to put the book back on the shelf, she followed Bracken from the room. They went upstairs to his workroom, and he handed her the new manuscript.

"That should keep you busy," he said with a small smile. "Why don't you meet me down by the pool in about an hour? I'm going to go over the outline of this last chapter first."

"All right. See you then." Summer left the room, walking slowly back down the hall to her own room, where she curled up in the middle of the bed and began to read the last book Bracken had had published.

She found the story so compelling that she almost

missed their swimming appointment. Glancing up at the mantel clock, she saw that she had three minutes to change and get down to the pool. She ran a hand through her short hair as she got up.

Changing into the scarlet bathing suit, she studied her image only briefly. She had selected the suit carefully, and she knew that it looked stunning on her small, shapely figure. The front of the one-piece suit was gathered at the middle, accenting her tiny waist, and the top hugged her firm breasts. She turned away from the mirror and looked over her shoulder; the back plunged provocatively low to mold to her rounded behind, and the thin, crisscrossed straps called attention to her smooth back. Pleased with the image, she hurried barefoot from the room.

She reached the stairs leading down to the first floor at the same time Bracken did, and she tried to keep from staring at him. His bathing suit left a lot less to the imagination than did hers, and Summer finally gave in to the temptation to scan his tall, muscled body. A thick mat of coppery hair covered his broad chest and long, muscular legs. Feeling her face flush with excitement, Summer started down the stairs. What on earth was wrong with her when she was around that man? It was indecent the way she reacted to his nearness!

She had reached the pool when she turned to see Bracken strolling unhurriedly down the final flight of stairs. Walking with a catlike grace, his muscles rippling with the movement, he stepped up on the diving board and dove into the water. Summer watched for a moment before she did the same. And to her astonishment, she found something else she did very well; she was a strong and excellent swimmer. Side by side, she and Bracken swam the distance of the pool twice, then climbed out.

Summer was laughing as Bracken handed her a towel. The water had been distracting and refreshing, and she felt vibrant and alive. Of course, she didn't need a swim to feel that way. Just standing so near Bracken had that exciting effect on her. She watched as he dried off, then turned away from her.

"Are you ready for a steam bath?" he asked, leading the way to the sauna.

She threw up her hands. "Tonight I'm ready for anything. I've found two things today that I can do, and I know I can conquer the sauna."

He ignored the last part of her statement. "Ready for anything?" he repeated, and she felt her breath catch in her throat. They both knew what he was alluding to, and Summer fell silent as he undid the latch on the sauna door.

Summer stepped inside the steamy room. An open pit of hot coals was smoldering, and Bracken threw a dipper of water on them, creating a fresh cloud of steam. The room was quite large, and he climbed up on the second tier of boards and stretched out on his towel. Following his lead, Summer lay down her towel and stretched out on the lower tier.

In moments she felt the perspiration bead up on her body as she relaxed totally. She lay very still, enjoying the feeling of tension draining away. It wasn't until she heard Bracken stir above her a couple of minutes later that she opened her eyes.

Climbing down from his bench, he sat on the very edge of hers. "How are you feeling?" he asked in a low voice. "Are the aching muscles easing?"

"Mmmm," she murmured; "the steam feels wonderful. I think I could lie here all night."

His laughter was low and husky. "No, you couldn't. The sauna enervates you after a short time. People who overdo are prone to lightheadedness and exhaustion."

"Really?" she asked, sitting up beside him. "It feels so heavenly."

"Really," he said, moving closer to her and reaching out to turn her so that her back was toward him. Slowly and sensuously, Bracken began to massage her back muscles with strong, caressing fingers. A delicious shiver raced over her body.

"You can't be cold," he murmured, his lips near her ear.

"No. No, I'm not cold," she stammered.

Bracken continued to caress her back, shoulders, and neck until she thought she would go crazy from the tingling sensations throughout her body.

"Lie down on your stomach and stretch out," he instructed, his hands continuing to knead her tender flesh.

Summer turned to look over her shoulder at him. She had had all of his tantalizing nearness she could stand for one night, but when he motioned for her to lie down, she hadn't the will power to resist him. Doing as she was told, she stretched out on the towel, turning her head to one side so that she could see him through the steamy mist. Didn't he know that he was driving her wild with his skilled hands? Didn't he know that she was in love with him? Couldn't he tell that she felt a fire in her veins when he touched her?

She gasped softly as his hands trailed down her body to the sensitive skin on her legs. Gently, ever so gently, he made caressing circles down the length of them, and Summer thought she would perish with the sweet agony.

"Feel good?" he murmured in a husky voice.

Summer swallowed hard, trying to find her voice and hoping it would sound casual and appreciative of his efforts. To her horror, the words came out in a husky caress. "Yes, it feels very good."

His hands stopped their movement, and she felt his body heat as he leaned over her, his lips soft on the moist skin of her neck. She moaned softly, and she heard Bracken whisper, "We've stayed long enough. I think it's time we called it a night."

Summer felt herself trembling as he helped her up from

the bench. She didn't know if her legs would support her, and it wasn't from the effect of too much time in the steamy room. Bracken held her hand as he led her to the door. When he opened it to usher her out, the blast of cool air that greeted her had an immediate, sobering effect. Summer blinked, staring out over the pool as though she were shocked that everything outside the sauna was the same as it had been before. It seemed that the whole world had changed there in that hazy mist under the delicious torment of Bracken's clever, smooth hands.

"Are you all right?" he asked, noticing her hesitation.

"Fine," she said, trying to sound casual, but she knew that no matter who she really was, she would never be fine again unless she could have Bracken Bohannon for herself, forever.

Neither of them spoke as they walked back up to the living room, and then up to the bedrooms. Summer wasn't even aware of what she was doing. Her mind was spinning as she wondered if Bracken intended to leave her at her door.

She didn't know whether to be disappointed or relieved when he murmured goodnight and turned to stroll down the hall. She watched until his strongly defined body had vanished, then went to the bathroom and took a cool shower.

When she returned to her room, she slipped into the tee shirt Bracken had given her and lay down on her bed with the book she was reading. She had forgotten that she wanted to read the current manuscript; she was involved in the story in his last book, and she turned to the page where she had stopped reading. Even that held her interest only briefly. Placing the book on the nightstand, she turned out her light and sighed, reliving once again every sensual stroke of Bracken's hands on her body. She shivered as she slipped into a deep sleep.

* * *

A short time later, she awakened with a jolt. That was it! There was the connection. It had come to her so vividly in a dream. She knew where she lived! Somehow she had remembered! It would solve everything, and it was so nearby. She lived in Monterey! Thirty miles away from Bracken! Filled with frantic excitement, Summer scooted from her bed and raced down the hall to Bracken's room.

"Bracken! Bracken!" she cried, flinging the door open.

He woke up immediately, sitting up in bed and flipping on the bedside lamp. "What's wrong?"

"I remember where I live! I remember, Bracken! It came to me in a dream."

He studied her feverish face for a moment, and his eyes were unreadable, but Summer had the feeling that he didn't share her excitement. "Are you sure?"

"Yes!" she exclaimed. "Oh, Bracken, I live in Monterey!"

"Monterey?" he repeated.

"Yes," she cried, rushing over to his bed and climbing on top of the covers. "Thank God! Thank God! I've remembered. Hurry! Hurry, Bracken. Get up. We have to go there right now."

He looked at the clock. "It's after eleven. Perhaps we should wait until morning." Summer didn't notice that he seemed almost reluctant to join in her excitement.

"No! No, I wouldn't sleep a wink. I have to go and find out for sure right now."

"Where in Monterey?"

For a moment the question almost sobered her. "I don't know," she admitted reluctantly. "I mean, I don't know what street, but I'm sure we can find it. I saw the house perfectly. It's a single-story white stucco with red tile, a split-rail fence with red roses, and a large shade tree in front."

"But you don't know which street?"

She shook her head, but her exuberance could not be tamed. "We'll find it. Hurry and get dressed."

"Summer, not tonight. It's foolish. Wait until tomorrow morning, when we can see something. We have little enough to go on as it is."

Her blue eyes suddenly glistened with tears. "Please, Bracken. Maybe I'll remember more when I get there. You don't know how it is to be in my situation. This is the first real hope I've had."

He scrutinized her clothing. "Are you going like that?" he drawled unexpectedly.

Summer stared down at her attire, aware for the first time since she had run from her bedroom of the tee shirt and the way it clung to her body. "Oh," she cried. "No, I'll get dressed. But hurry. I'll only be a minute."

Bracken shoved the covers aside, and before he could get out of bed, Summer fled back to her own room. She was filled with jubilation. The pieces of the puzzle were falling into place. She would have an identity soon.

She pulled on her jeans, blouse, and jacket, remembering only at the last moment to put on shoes. She was back in Bracken's room before he had finished buttoning his shirt. She watched in fevered anxiety as he pulled a jacket from his closet and slipped into it.

Summer gasped when they opened the door to leave the house. Rose and Harry were getting ready to enter, and for a moment they all looked at each other awkwardly.

"Did you enjoy your evening?" Bracken asked as though there were nothing odd about him and Summer leaving the house so late.

"Yes, we did," Rose said, her expression curious.

"Well, don't just stand there woman," Bracken joked. "Come on into the house. We're just leaving."

"So it seems," Rose murmured dryly. "Little late for an outing, isn't it? Is everything all right?"

Bracken laughed lightly, downplaying Summer's frantic mood. "It seems that Summer can't sleep, and I thought a ride might be good for her."

"I see," Rose grunted, nodding her head, but it was plain that the whole situation seemed peculiar to her. Brushing past Bracken and Summer, she and Harry entered the house. "Drive carefully," she said as a parting comment before she and Harry disappeared up the steps. Summer could hear the couple whispering to each other, but she was oblivious to the way her late night departure with Bracken seemed. She had to find the house, for in it lay the key to her past.

Tugging at his hand, she hurried him toward the car. He looked at Summer thoughtfully before he put the vehicle into gear; he seemed to have something he wanted to say to her, but, instead, he shook his head wearily, turned on the car lights and drove down the hill.

Summer was fidgeting and wiggling in her seat, wanting to urge Bracken to drive faster, but even in her anxiety she realized that it would do them no good to become involved in an accident because of her wild desire to reach her destination. She glanced at Bracken's rigid profile, barely able to make out the lines of his face, and she was surprised to see how tightly closed his mouth was. Looking back at the road, she didn't give herself a chance to puzzle over his grim countenance.

It seemed like an eternity to Summer, but they finally reached Monterey, and Bracken, sighing at the monumental task before him, turned into a residential district bordering the coastline. Slowly, he cruised down the street, giving Summer a chance to survey the neat rows of lovely houses standing in the shadows of the street lights.

"It wasn't near the sea," she murmured, a frown

marring her pretty features. "That will save us some time. It wasn't near any water. I'm sure it wasn't."

Without a word, Bracken drove out of the tract and traveled to another area of town. Again he drove slowly down the long, winding streets, giving Summer ample time to view the assortment of houses. She glanced quickly over them, shaking her head and urging him to drive on. She had to find the right street, and she knew she would recognize her house in an instant when she saw it. The picture held fast in her mind, and she memorized the shape of the house and the lovely rosebushes growing on the fence. There was a shade tree in the front yard, and grass. Yes, she knew she would recognize it in a moment, and she felt excitement run through her like wildfire at the thought.

"Go faster," she implored, turning to Bracken, frustrated at the delay.

Glancing at her, Bracken spoke in hard tones. "Summer, in all probability we won't find this house until we comb the whole city. Do you realize how many streets we could cover before you spotted it? Do you know how big this city is? This is foolish. Wait until tomorrow morning when we can at least see properly. Be reasonable."

Summer experienced a panicky feeling at the thought that he might turn back. She was in no mood to be reasonable—not when there was a chance that she might learn her identity. She shook her head stubbornly. "I can't wait until morning. Don't ask me to. If this image escapes me, I may never find out who I am. I know I'm asking a lot, Bracken, but I need your help now. I *must* find this house."

"Summer," he said wearily, "I want to help you, but this may not be the way or the time. Besides, you know that Ellen Story will show up eventually."

"I don't know a thing about Ellen Story," she cried. He couldn't turn back! She wouldn't let him turn back! "She could have vanished for all I know. Don't take me back to Isolation until I've had a decent chance to find my house. Please."

"All right," he conceded with a deep sigh. "We'll search awhile longer."

"Oh, thank you," she cried, moving closer to him and tracing his strong jaw with her fingertips. "Thank you."

He caught her hand and kissed her fingertips before releasing it. Summer blinked back rising tears as she leaned closer. He turned down another street. "Describe the house for me again."

Summer told him again, and the long search continued. They covered mile after mile of houses, and it was beginning to look futile even to Summer, who clung wildly to the image in her mind. She had to find it. She had to!

It was after one o'clock when she suddenly cried out in triumph. "There it is! I can't believe it! There it is. Look, Bracken. That house with the red-tiled roof."

Summer couldn't believe her eyes. They had found it! They had *finally* found it! The house fit the description in her mind exactly. Then, for just a moment, she felt her heart stop; instead of grass, the yard was covered in green rock. Buoying her sagging spirits again, she determined not to let such a minor detail ruin her jubilation. After all, she was struggling to remember anything at all, and she would stake her life that she lived in Monterey. She was as sure of that fact as she was that she was alive and breathing.

Bracken stopped the car in front of the house. "Are you positive that this is the one?"

Summer nodded vigorously. "This is the one," she breathed, her heart pounding wildly in her chest. "This is my house."

Bracken looked at his watch. "It's so late. We can come back in the morning. Your sudden appearance will be a shock to your family."

Summer clutched at him, her fingers biting into his shoulders as she looked into his face with frantic eyes. "No. Please! I'm going up to that door right now. Nothing can keep me from it."

Bracken drew a deep breath and removed her fingers from his shoulders. "Now try to calm down. You could be wrong about this house. What if you walk up there and the people don't know you?"

"They'll know me! I know they'll know me! This is my house." Pulling her hands from his, she turned with blind determination toward the door.

"I'll go with you," Bracken insisted. "But get control of yourself."

Summer opened the door and was startled when Bracken came up behind her, suddenly gripping her shoulders and shaking her furiously. "Summer," he commanded. "Calm down!"

His sharp voice was like a slap in the face, and she gazed up into his hard features. Then she closed her eyes for a moment and nodded. Taking several gulps of the cool night air, she forced herself to settle down. Then, with her trembling hand in Bracken's, she walked up to the front door.

With a shaking finger, Summer pressed the bell. Although there was a light on inside, it was several minutes before anyone came to the door, and even then it remained closed.

"Who's there?" an old man's voice called out.

Summer looked up at Bracken, wide-eyed. She didn't have a true name to give the man. "Please," she said, "I must talk to you."

"Who are you?" he asked again without opening the door. "It's one-thirty in the morning. What do you want?"

"Don't you recognize my voice?" Summer cried in desperation.

There was a pause, and then the door slowly opened.

Summer thought her heart would burst as she waited to see if she would recognize the man. Would he have the brown eyes she had thought she recognized when she looked at Harry for the first time? Would someone welcome her with open arms, hugs, and kisses?

A man in his seventies, short and bald, peered out at her over his bifocals. Behind him, clutching his arm, stood a tiny old woman, her hair twisted up in paper-wrapped pin curls, her cheeks smudged with a white night cream.

And they didn't recognize Summer any more than she recognized them. Her heart sank, and she bit down on her bottom lip until her teeth cut into it.

"Who are you?" the man repeated, staring up at Bracken as though he had been tricked into opening the door.

"My friend is suffering from amnesia," Bracken said in a calm voice. "She thought she remembered this house; she believed that it was her home. I'm terribly sorry to have disturbed you. If it hadn't been for the unusual circumstances, we never would have gotten you up so late. Do you recognize her? Do you know her at all?"

Both of the old people shook their heads. "We've been in this house for thirty years. We don't know her," the man said, a hint of suspicion still in his voice.

The woman was more sympathetic. "We're sorry, but we don't know you. We've never had children, and we don't keep up much with young folks."

Then they closed the door. Summer stood there for a moment staring at it in disbelief. She had been so sure that it was her house. She had been positive that someone in it would be happy to see her. But she had been wrong. Suddenly she turned and, stumbling down the sidewalk, ran back to the car, jerked the door open, and climbed inside.

Bracken was right behind her, quickly getting in on the driver's side. He pulled her to him, wrapping her in his arms. "I'm sorry, Summer," he murmured in a husky voice.

But Summer was too numb to reply. Tears brimming in her eyes, she stayed pressed close to Bracken for a long time, her arms hanging limply by her sides.

"Are you all right? Do you want to go home now?" he asked later, his lips near her ear, his breath warm on her face.

Summer whispered "yes" in a bitter little voice. She would go back to Isolation with Bracken, but she didn't have a home. She didn't belong anywhere. Not even with him.

Chapter Eight

Bracken helped Summer from the car, his arm protectively around her shoulders as they walked to the house, but even he didn't have the power to comfort her.

"How about a cup of coffee?" he asked, looking down at her with concerned eyes.

Summer nodded vaguely. She didn't care what she did. Automatically, she followed Bracken into the kitchen and watched as he prepared the coffee. Sitting down at the table across from him, she stared before her blindly, only half listening to what he was saying.

"We'll hunt for the house again tomorrow if you're sure you live in Monterey. And if you do live there, we'll find out where."

Summer nodded again, absently taking a sip of the steaming hot coffee. "Oh!" She winced when the liquid burned her mouth.

"Summer," Bracken said sharply, "pay attention to what you're doing. Summer, are you listening to me?"

She frowned as her eyes met his, then pursed her lips and blinked back a rush of fresh tears. "Oh, Bracken, I was so sure . . . so sure," she whispered. "I would have staked my life that that was the house." She shook her head. "I don't know how I could have been so wrong about it."

He pulled a white handkerchief from his breast pocket and handed it to her, watching as she dabbed at the tears, a sob catching in her throat.

"We'll look again tomorrow," he repeated reassuringly. She nodded, looking up at him with red-rimmed eyes, but, in truth, she didn't think she had the heart to suffer such a paralyzing defeat again.

Bracken finished his coffee and, seeing that Summer wasn't really interested in hers, suggested that they go up to bed. Like an automaton, she stood and trailed behind him up the stairs.

Bracken opened her door for her. "If you want me, just call," he said quietly. Then he bent his head and touched her forehead briefly with his warm lips.

Summer paused for a moment before she opened her bedroom door and went inside. Numbly, she changed into the tee shirt and climbed into bed. For several minutes she lay staring up at the skylight, wondering how the image of the white house with the red tile had failed her so utterly. Were there several houses like hers? What were the odds against such a possibility? Two such houses in Monterey? With a tall tree and a fence with roses? The tears began to rush from her eyes. When would it all end? How long could she endure the uncertainty of her position? Rolling over on her stomach, she buried her face in her pillow to muffle the sobs and wept bitterly at her cruel disappointment.

She didn't hear the door open and was unaware that Bracken had come in. Silently slipping into bed beside her, he pulled her into his arms and held her head against his shoulder as her tears fell. Gently, he pressed her trembling body against his warmth, caressing her back and shoulders and crooning words of consolation.

Summer didn't know when she stopped crying. Turning her face up to look at Bracken, she gasped as his lips lowered to hers in a soft, lingering kiss. She wrapped her arms around his broad back and pulled him possessively to her. As they lay on their sides facing each other, their bodies pressed tightly together, she realized that Bracken wore nothing besides his pajama bottoms.

His kiss intensified and his knowing hands roamed freely over her body. She felt the searching warmth of his fingers on her bare skin as he found his way under her tee shirt. His fingertips brushed across the tender skin of her quivering stomach, and she felt a fire leap inside her. The teasing caress traveled upward, and Summer moaned as his hand found the softness of her breast and cupped it. He pressed her back against the bed, and she pulled his head down to her throat. His lips explored the sensitive column, and Summer arched her neck to further expose it to his touch. All the while his fingers played with the taut nipple of her breast, teasing it into a hard awareness. She wanted to lose her unhappiness in the burning fire of Bracken's love.

A soft gasp escaped her parted lips at the dancing flames he aroused in her hungry body. She felt her passion soar to new heights, and she longed for the satisfaction that only his touch could bring. But she was cruelly disappointed. She barely understood the hoarse words he murmured against her pulsating throat.

"Not now, my darling. Not when you're so upset and vulnerable. When I take you, I want you to be fully aware of what it means, of the consequences of your action." With that thick, muffled explanation, he pulled away slightly and, his hands resting on her back, held her gently, lending her his warmth.

Summer was stunned for a moment, but she lay quietly in his arms, breathing raggedly. She had too much pride to protest the abrupt cessation of his lovemaking. It was agony to be held so near him and not to have him. For several moments he lay there holding her, stroking her hair, before she realized that she had forgotten all about the misery of the futile search for her home.

Summer didn't know how it happened, but presently her heart slowed, her raging desire subsided, and she was lulled to sleep in Bracken's arms. It was a deep and completely relaxing sleep, and she was untroubled by dreams.

Some time in the night she awakened, startled and unsure of what had disturbed her. When she realized that she was still being held in those strong, comforting arms, she lay very still, trying to get her bearings, wanting to know why she had come awake so abruptly. Slowly it dawned on her; Bracken had murmured something in a tortured voice. And that something was Marissa's name!

Summer lay there in quiet desperation for a moment longer. So, even when he held another woman in his arms, it was still Marissa whom he thought of. She had known how much he must have loved her—he had kept her room as a shrine—but she had dared to believe, to hope, though she knew about Darlene, that Bracken might come to care for her in more than a physical way. And she had been wrong. When she could bear her tormented thoughts no longer, she eased from his arms and crept to the very edge of the bed. And there she lay, huddled in a desolate ball, dipping in and out of a tortured sleep, until a brilliant sun scattered sunshine through the skylight.

Jolting awake, Summer looked at the other side of the bed. It was empty now; Bracken had stolen away. She breathed a sigh of relief and lay back against the pillows. She would hold the bitter lesson she had learned in her heart; no matter what her situation, she would not fall into

Bracken's arms again. She had enough agony and heartache without giving herself to a man who didn't, who couldn't, love her. She coaxed herself from her bed, and pulling on the huge man's robe, she staggered down the hall to the shower.

Some time later she appeared at the breakfast table, a determined smile on her face, but Bracken wasn't there.

Summer glanced at the archway as Rose walked in from the kitchen. "You eating this morning, or are you going to be like Bracken and just ask for toast and coffee after I picked strawberries for waffles?" the housekeeper demanded. "The berries are the first from the garden this season," she added as an incentive.

Summer kept the smile on her lips as she looked at Rose's hard face. She had long ago realized that the woman couldn't intimidate a butterfly; she really didn't want breakfast, but she was unwilling to disappoint Rose.

"I'd love some strawberry waffles," she declared with a pretense of cheerfulness.

Rose gave her a doubtful look, but a slow smile of satisfaction curved her thin lips before she turned back to the kitchen.

After Rose had served her, Summer was glad she had decided to eat breakfast. The waffles were delicious, and they settled her quivering stomach. After she had lingered over a third cup of coffee she asked, "Rose, where's Bracken?"

"Working."

"Did he ask for me this morning?" Summer inquired hesitantly.

Rose shook her head. "No. In fact, he told me to let you sleep." Rose winked. "I said to myself that the two of you must have had quite a ride last night, but then Mr. Bohannon acted kind of irritable, not wanting breakfast and all, so I said to myself that maybe you hadn't had such a nice time after all."

If she had expected Summer to confide anything about the previous evening, Rose was disappointed. Summer was pondering whether to go up to Bracken's workroom to type, but in the end she came to the conclusion that she couldn't face him. Not after what had happened in her bedroom last night. And maybe he didn't want to face her either.

"I think I'll take a walk in the woods this morning," Summer said impulsively, looking out the window. Now that she had thought of it, the idea sounded appealing. The sun was out, and the day looked warm.

Suddenly Devil came thundering into the kitchen, wagging his nub of a tail. Summer looked down at him in surprise. "Well, hello, boy. What brings you running?"

Rose narrowed her eyes at the animal. "You said walk, and he thought you meant him." She shook a skinny finger at Devil. "Harry's already taken you for your walk today and well you know it."

"Oh, can I take him with me?" Summer asked, thinking that she would enjoy some company.

"Might be a good idea," Rose said. "It's easy to get lost in these woods. You should stay near the house."

"I don't intend to go far," Summer assured her. "I don't want to lose my way. And I won't be gone long. Will I need to use a leash for Devil?"

"No. He'll run alongside you. He just likes to go along. Mr. Bo doesn't let him run free over the grounds because he's afraid something will happen to him, what with wild animals and the like. But he'll stay within earshot of you. Mr. Bo has trained him not to stray far."

"Okay. We'll see you later then." Deciding that she didn't need a jacket, Summer left the house, setting out on her walk with Devil running beside her.

The day was glorious, and Summer tramped along the trail, watching the sunlight dance as it streamed down through the leaves and branches, delighting in the sights of the colorful spring flowers. Once she stopped to pick a deep purple iris, holding its velvet beauty near her face to study the yellow veined petals. She laughed at Devil's antics as he busied himself exploring the ground, sniffing and running about when he thought he had discovered something interesting in a hole or under a mound of debris.

Determined not to dwell on last night's events, Summer lost herself in the lushness and the diversity of the forest. She occasionally looked over her shoulder, making sure that she wasn't going too far or losing her way. The woods were very peaceful and pleasant, the solitude punctuated only by the natural sounds of the forest animals and the wind. The shrill squawk of a blue jay would catch her attention every so often, and once in a while Devil would send a squirrel or a woodrat running for cover, startling both Summer and the little animal out of their contentment in the warmth of the spring day.

But slowly, insidiously, the unhappy reality of her predicament crept into Summer's mind to destroy her tranquillity. She had learned nothing at all about herself. The memories she had believed in had proved wrong. The love she had found had proved impossible. Her future was as bleak as it had been since she had had the accident. And where was there to go from here?

Summer became so preoccupied with her thoughts that she lost all sense of time and place. She walked until she felt exhausted. And it wasn't until she sat down wearily on a stump that she realized that she didn't know how much time had passed, or how far into the forest she had gone. Devil slumped down in front of her with a tired grunt. Shielding her eyes with her hand, Summer gazed up through the tall trees at the sun.

To her surprise, it was high in the sky! She looked back down at Devil; his eyelids were drooping, and his tongue was hanging out the side of his mouth as he lay panting heavily. He was thirsty, Summer realized guiltily. And so was she, now that she thought of it, and she was hungry, too. Her thoughts had gotten her into trouble again, no matter how good her intentions had been. And poor Devil, who had come along to keep her company, was paying for it.

She turned her head, looking around her. Her neck muscles were tense, and her legs were tingling now that she was sitting down. She knew that she was fatigued, and she really was very thirsty. She didn't think she could possibly have traveled anywhere near as far on foot as she and Bracken had gone on horseback, but still she wondered if there might be a stream nearby. The big one she and Bracken had eaten lunch by yesterday must run down through the hills somewhere. She sighed, almost too weary to bother to look for it. Yet, if she didn't, she would get dehydrated on the walk back.

Rolling over on his side, Devil looked at her once, then closed his bright eyes, his tongue lolling.

Summer forced herself up to stretch her taut muscles. "C'mon, boy," she urged. "Want a drink? Go get the water."

She had no idea if the animal would know what she was talking about, or how much of a chance she was taking giving the command, but she felt it was worth a try.

Immediately, Devil bounded up as though he weren't tired at all and, wagging his tail, galloped farther into the dense forest, causing a covey of quail to rise upward as he plunged into their domain. He paused only briefly to watch the commotion, then pursued his course.

Summer was barely able to keep him in sight, much less keep up with him. She was breathing hard as she hurried behind him. One minute she had him in sight, and the next minute he was gone! Looking about frantically, she started to call out to him when he charged back through the undergrowth, water dribbling down his chin and dripping from his heavy jowls.

"That's a good boy," Summer said, immensely relieved to see him. "Go get the water." She kept up with him this time, emerging from the dense bushes to find tall trees overhanging a small, sparkling stream that ran down a hillside. Gratefully, she bent down on stiff knees and scooped up a handful of the cool, crystal clear mountain water. She took several drinks before her thirst was satisfied, then, Devil by her side, she found a soft bed of leaves and lay down to rest. Breathing heavily from weariness, she looked up at the sun glinting through the trees and closed her eyes.

Summer's heart was pounding ominously when she awakened in fright. Devil was growling menacingly at something. For a moment she was petrified. Something had her in its grip! She was being forced to the ground by the strength of a savage, hairy weight, and she was too terrified to look for fear of making the nightmare real. Barely daring to breathe, she shivered violently as she forced her eyes open.

Her groan of relief was plainly audible in the quiet forest. Devil was lying protectively across her legs, guarding her from the menace of a busy family of skunks, who happened to be arriving at the stream for an afternoon drink. Summer stared up through the trees at the sun again, and she was alarmed to see that it was dipping toward the earth; she and Devil had been out in the woods for hours! Rose would be worried if they didn't return soon. She had foolishly told the housekeeper that she wouldn't be gone long, and she really hadn't intended to be, but the silence of the forest and her own whirling thoughts had distorted her sense of the here and now.

Pushing Devil off her legs, Summer tried to stand. She was so stiff and cramped that she didn't know if it would be possible. She had stupidly overexerted herself, and Devil's weight on her legs had numbed them. She cursed herself for wasting so much time. Devil was still standing guard, growling at the skunks, seeming to know instinctively, or perhaps from past experience, that he shouldn't get too close to the fluffy little animals, but the skunks paid the intruders little mind. They drank from the stream, then mama skunk and her babies ambled about their business in the afternoon sun.

Summer finally managed to get her cramped body in motion, and, ignoring the grumbling in her stomach, headed away from the stream. Suddenly she stopped dead still in her tracks. She had no idea which way to go! She was lost!

Sensing her anxiety, Devil looked up at her and whined. He was eager to be on his way, but Summer didn't know which way that was. She stood there for a while, trying to get her bearings, but the truth was that she didn't know one direction from another. She hadn't intended to travel into the forest so far that she couldn't find her way back to the well-traveled path she had first been on. Her heart sank when she remembered that she had lost the path even before she had sent Devil to the stream. She had forgotten to pay attention! Oh, which way should she go? How could she have been such a fool—and after she had been warned about getting lost in the forest, too! Fighting back futile tears of frustration, she started walking, hoping, praying that she was headed in the right direction, but she had no way of knowing.

As he trotted along beside her, Devil began to grow restless. Summer wondered if he, too, was tired and distressed by her foolishness. Was he ready to bolt away on his own and abandon her to the dense forest? Rose had said that he would stay by her side, but he gave every indication of going his own way. Then it occured to her that, just as he had known how to find the stream, he probably knew his way home. Why hadn't she thought of it before?

"Home, Devil!" she commanded, hoping the order wasn't as ridiculous as it sounded. "Go, boy. Go to Bracken."

Devil gave an excited bark, and again Summer wondered if she was being foolish to give the animal his freedom. He plunged away in a moment, eager to run, and Summer was left to struggle with thick bushes, low-hanging trees, briars, and aching muscles as she straggled behind him, barely keeping him in sight. At last she could keep up no longer, and, tears rising to her eyes, she watched as Devil vanished into the trees.

"Devil! Devil!" she called desperately. "Come back here!" But the animal paid no heed, either beyond hearing or beyond caring. His destination in mind, he left Summer far behind while he ran through the forest.

Summer slumped down on a mat of brown leaves. What now? she wondered tiredly. Surely she had been missed at the house, and someone would come to hunt for her before nightfall. She debated about whether to go on or wait there. She knew that Devil had probably been headed in the right direction, and she was closer to Isolation than she might be if she attempted to push through the forest on her own.

A tear slipped from her eye. She would sit here and wait and hope and be red-faced when someone finally came. *If* someone came. If Devil returned to the house. It seemed that not only was she plagued with no memory, no past, and no future, but she was lacking in good sense, too.

She was massaging her stiff neck with equally stiff fingers when Devil came running back to her. And right behind him stalked Bracken. A savage-faced, furious Bracken.

Summer sucked in her breath at the sight of her rescuer. He was angry, there was no doubt about that. He had obviously endured as much of her as he could take in one lifetime. He had left his study to come hunt for her, and she knew that today he had said he—they—would have to put in a full day of work. Well, she thought defensively, he should have woken her and insisted that she come with him; then she wouldn't be out here in these woods lost like some dang fool with half a brain. She bit down on her trembling lower lip to still it.

"What's wrong with you?" he demanded harshly as he approached. "What kind of fool stunt is this? Has anyone told you that you need a guard?"

Though possibly deserved, his hostile words angered her. She didn't want to be out here in these woods, and she didn't want him to be her guard. "Not that I know of, but then, I wouldn't really remember, would I?" she snapped crossly.

"Why the devil don't you come back to the house?" he barked. "What are you doing sitting here all day? Rose didn't expect you to be gone long, and I didn't know what to think when Devil returned alone."

"You could have thought I was lost!" she hissed. "Would I be sitting here otherwise?"

"Beats me if I know," he declared. "You've been gone for hours, and now I find you sitting here."

"Stop it!" she cried. "I didn't want you to find me here, but I lost my way, and your wonderful dog just ran off and left me." It wasn't quite the truth; she had told Devil to go home, but he needn't have run so fast.

"You lost your way?" he mocked.

Suddenly he yanked her up from the ground, unaware of and unconcerned about her throbbing, aching body as he marched her out of the trees. And on the other side of the thicket and tall trees, a short distance away, were the fence and stable. Beyond them was the vegetable garden. Isolation was, of course, no more than three hundred feet away!

Exhausted and embarrassed, she began to laugh.

"We went all the way to the stream for a drink," she explained between nervous giggles, "and then I couldn't find my way back out of the forest. I didn't know how to get back to the house. I couldn't find my way. We had walked for a long time, and I had fallen asleep, and—"

Bracken shook his head in disgust, but Summer saw the hard lines of his face soften. "You must have walked in circles. The small stream is about a mile from here. The path leads to a cluster of scrub oaks, and the water is directly through those trees." He wrapped an arm around her shoulders and began to walk with her back to the house. "You're going to be the death of me yet."

Summer's laughter gave way to building tears at his change of disposition, and no matter how much she fought against them, they began to slide down her dirt-streaked face.

Bracken turned to stare at her. "What's wrong now?"

"I didn't mean to get lost," she murmured, a sob almost choking her.

Bracken swung her up into his arms and hugged her slender body to his. "You poor baby," he murmured, cradling her head on his shoulder. "You do have a time of it."

Summer tensed in his arms, though she wanted nothing more than to be held close to his warm body. His ragged voice and the way he had called out Marissa's name in the night sounded in her head, and she refused to yield to the betraying emotions she felt when he held her. She looked back at the forest, rather than his face, as he carried her into the house.

He didn't put her on her feet until he had taken her into one of the upstairs baths. "Soak in a tub of hot water, then come down and eat. I'll have Rose hurry with dinner. You must be starving; it's after three."

Summer nodded, pressing her lips tightly together to

keep her tears at bay. She remained still until Bracken had gone, gently closing the door. Then she stripped off her clothes, turned the taps on full, and climbed into the tub.

Summer soaked her aching muscles as long as she dared; she didn't want Rose to rush dinner, then have to keep it waiting for her. Still tired, but feeling a little better, she wrapped herself in a big towel and went to her room. Then she changed into the blue slacks and a white blouse, which was loose enough to be comfortable.

She was happy to find that Rose had prepared a very simple meal of hamburgers with lettuce, tomatoes, and pickles, French fries, and soda. Junk food, she thought with a wan smile, and a memory tugged at her consciousness. Her father had always told her that junk food wasn't nutritious, but she loved it all the same.

Bracken turned around in time to catch the smile that lingered on her lips. "Ah, I see you're feeling better, pathfinder," he joked.

"That's the name of a book, isn't it?" she asked seriously. "I think I did a paper on it when I went to the university."

"Oh," he said. "And where was that?"

"Why, in Monterey. I went to the university in Monterey."

"I see," he murmured. "And?"

She shrugged, her mind closing off the short fountain of information that had spouted so briefly. "And that's all I remember," she said with a sigh.

"Which university did you attend?" he asked.

"The state university in Monterey," she said emphatically. "I did go. I'm sure of it," she insisted.

He didn't say anything else, and she glared at him, challenging him to deny it. "I did go!"

"You didn't go in Monterey," he said quietly. "There is no university in Monterey—only a junior college."

Summer dropped down in a chair. She had been so sure

she had gone to the university in Monterey. But then, she had been sure that her home was in Monterey, too.

"I see," she said meekly. Then, feeling depressed, she took a bite of her hamburger and stared out the window at the hills beyond. It seemed that the bits and pieces that were surfacing weren't accurate at all. Was there really a blond man in her past? Was there really an older man with brown eyes? Was there really a dark woman who had laughed at her?

Summer drew a deep breath and let it slip through her parted lips. Sometimes she wondered if it was all only a nightmare. Sometimes she wondered if she was even real.

Chapter Nine

Sunday morning after breakfast, Bracken informed Summer that the cookout would take place at two in the afternoon, and she was invited if she wanted to go with him. She decided that an outing might be good for her, and she accepted gratefully.

"Be ready about one-thirty," he told her, watching as she got up from the table and started toward the stairs.

"All right." She wanted to spend the rest of the morning reading Bracken's book. She hoped it would take her mind off her own troubles. She laughed unhappily to herself, thinking of the irony. The source of her problems was her lack of memory, and here she was wanting to keep from thinking about it when she should try to remember anything she could.

Without looking back, she trailed up the steps to her room. She sighed as she lay down on the bed with Bracken's last book. She knew that she was only reading it to try to learn something about Bracken's relationship with his dead wife. Why had she fallen in love with him? He obviously couldn't be true to anyone, and not only would a woman have to compete with other women to hold Bracken's interest, she would also have to cope with his career. Summer smiled a grim smile; she was proud that he was a writer and that he took pride in his craft. The writing would be no problem for her, but she could never, never cope with Bracken having other women.

"You silly, silly goose," she said aloud. What on earth was she doing, lying there speculating on a relationship that didn't even exist? Bracken had made no advances to her since he had carried her out of the forest. And she didn't know what ties she had to a man in her past. Why did she persist in pursuing her fantasies about Bracken Bohannon? Was she so simple that she didn't see that they had no future together, or was she so much in love with him that her foolish heart wouldn't let the dream die?

Opening the book, she began to read.

The time passed rapidly, and, finishing the last page, Summer laid the book down on the bed and stared up at the skylight. She had learned nothing tangible about Bracken's relationship with his wife, but from his writing she could tell that he was a man of deep and lasting passions; he loved hard and he loved fully. She puzzled over it for several minutes, for it seemed unreasonable that such a man should indulge in affairs outside his marriage. Oh, stop it! she told herself angrily. The book was a work of fiction; she was fooling herself to think she could find something of the real man in such a work.

Placing the book carefully on the bedside table, she got up to change her clothes for the cookout. It did sound like fun, and she began to get excited about it. After slipping into her slacks and a yellow blouse, she stepped into her loafers, ran her fingers through her wispy curls, and hurried downstairs.

Bracken was waiting for her, lounging on the couch. She

smiled when she saw him, and he smiled back as he stood up. "Ready?"

"Yes," she said, giving a slight nod of her head.

He held out his hand to her. "Then let's go."

Summer despised the way her hand trembled as she slipped it into Bracken's, and she was glad when he released it as they got into the car.

The ride to the house where the barbecue was held was a short one, and Summer was surprised to find that the food was already being cooked when she and Bracken arrived. The delicious aroma of char-broiled hot dogs and hamburgers drifted toward them as they left the car and walked around to the backyard where the preparations were under way. Tables laden with food were arranged around two large brick barbecues, and people were already milling around the tables, dressing their hot dogs and hamburgers and scooping up big spoonfuls of baked beans and potato salad.

Bracken grinned at Summer. "Does the sight of all that food make you hungry?"

"The smell *and* the sight," she said, looking just a bit apprehensively at the group of strangers.

"Let's dig in then," he insisted.

"But I thought the cookout wasn't supposed to begin until two o'clock," she said.

Bracken shrugged his broad shoulders. "We're all friends here. We don't stand on ceremony. If the neighbors arrive, then the celebration gets under way."

"I'm ready," she said with a laugh, watching as a man drew himself a beer from a big keg set up at one end of the table nearest them.

Summer and Bracken picked up paper plates and began to heap food on them as they went down the buffet line, deciding that every item they passed looked too good to miss. They were chatting and laughing gaily when Summer moved away from the table and heard Darlene's voice.

"Over here, Bracken," the woman called out. "I've saved a place for you."

Oh, no, not again, Summer thought, but she had no choice but to force a smile to her quivering lips and follow Bracken to the nearly empty table where Darlene sat. The reporter managed to look sleek and polished even in jeans, and Summer's heart sank at the expectation of an uneasy afternoon in her company.

"What do you want to drink, Summer?" Bracken asked, setting down his plate beside Darlene's. "I'll get the beverages. No, don't tell me," he said when Summer started to speak, "I remember. A soda, right?"

"Yes," she said, putting as much cheerfulness into the word as she could muster.

"That's convenient—that he's gone for a minute, I mean," Darlene said, turning to face Summer. It crossed Summer's mind that the afternoon might be even more unpleasant than she had imagined when the woman's eyes sparked with hatred. "This convalescent scene is getting to be old hat, *cousin,*" she drawled maliciously. "If you're convalescing, shouldn't you be home in bed? And if you're well, shouldn't you get on about your business, whatever it is?"

For a few seconds, Summer was too stunned to speak.

Darlene filled in the gap. "If you have any intentions of being more than a cousin to Bracken, let me advise you right here and now to forget them. If anybody lays a claim to Bracken Bohannon, it will be me."

Summer stared at Darlene's angry features for a minute, wanting to lash out, wanting to take her uncertainty and unhappiness out on the sleek brunette, but she knew it was futile. "Aren't you overreacting to a little old cousin?" she asked with mock innocence.

Darlene started to reply, but Bracken appeared with the drinks, and she directed her comments to him instead of to Summer.

The afternoon passed quickly, much to Summer's surprise. There were games, three-legged races, arm wrestling, apple bobbing, and other such pursuits, but Summer found that Darlene and her comments about Bracken had dampened the day. Was it apparent to Darlene that Summer was in love with Bracken, or was she just exhibiting a possessive jealousy, protecting her property in case it was in dispute? Summer was glad when the day was over, and she and Bracken returned to Isolation.

She lingered in the living room for only a few minutes before excusing herself to go to her room. Lying down on her bed, she picked up another of Bracken's books; it held her interest until she drifted off into a troubled sleep.

The next morning Bracken decided that Summer should go into Monterey so Dr. Dickerson could take the stitches out of her head. It had been over a week since the accident, and the wound had healed nicely. The only thing that hadn't healed was Summer's memory, and it was beginning to seem that it would never do so. After she had been wrong about the university in Monterey, she had stopped trying to raise memories from her mind. Why should she bother? The "facts" that surfaced had no basis, no existence, so what was she to believe in? She clung to the thought that Ellen Story would return to her apartment and solve the mystery. After the Monterey disappointments, Summer was left with no other hope.

Bracken had a deadline to meet with the new book, so Rose was enlisted to drive Summer into town. The housekeeper wasn't much of a talker, but she was pleasant enough company.

When Summer entered the doctor's office, Rose went with her. The doctor removed the stitches and told her that the wound had healed nicely, but when Summer asked about her memory, he could only shake his head sympathetically. He could no more predict when the faulty mechanism would correct itself than Summer could, and he couldn't account for the fictitious facts that had surfaced. He conceded that generally the information one remembered had some basis in fact; he patted her hand reassuringly and told her not to despair.

He assured her that her memory would eventually return; all the odds were in her favor. Something usually triggered the memory sooner or later in cases like hers. He suggested that she give herself another month, but then, if nothing surfaced, they would discuss therapy. Summer thanked him and left, not at all heartened.

Rose smiled at her as they left the office, and when she saw Summer's sad face and weak smile, she insisted that they have a nice lunch in a nearby restaurant. Summer wasn't very hungry, but she didn't want to be unappreciative of Rose's efforts to cheer her, so she agreed. Perhaps it would perk up her sagging spirits.

Rose parked the car in front of a pretty little blue-and-white building. As they walked by the window on the way to the entrance, Summer looked into the room, staring at the quaint blue-and-white checkered tablecloths. Her gaze riveted itself to one table in particular, and she gave a little gasp; a man with blond hair just like the man in her mind was sitting at the table, watching a waitress stroll by on shapely legs. He turned to look out the window, and Summer froze where she stood. It was Desmond! It was the blond man she had seen so often in her head over the past week. Her eyes locked with his, and she saw amazement written on his face as he stood up, knocking over a cup of coffee in the process.

Summer couldn't move. She watched in fascination as the man ran toward the door, opened it, and rushed out onto the sidewalk. She could hear the shock and confusion in Rose's voice as he touched Summer's shoulder, but she couldn't make heads or tails of what the poor woman was saying. She was mesmerized by the man before her, and her heart beat wildly in anxious expectation.

"Ree!" he cried. "Oh, Ree! Where have you been? I've looked everywhere. I've combed heaven and earth to find you!"

Summer stared blankly at him. She knew no more about him now that he had spoken and stood there before her than she had known before. She was sure he was the blond man in her past, but other than that fact, there was nothing that sparked in her memory. The realization was a stunning disappointment, but at least he seemed to know her.

Grasping her by the shoulders, he shook her roughly as though the motion had the power to make her speak. "Say something to me, Rebecca! Don't hate me!"

"I—I don't hate you," she whispered in response. In fact, she felt nothing at all for him, and she was shattered that seeing him hadn't caused her to remember everything. His appearance had triggered nothing beyond the initial shock of connecting his face with the one that had haunted her. "I don't . . .I'm afraid I don't know who you are," she confessed breathlessly, "but thank heavens you know me! Who am I?"

Penetrating blue eyes stared momentarily into hers as the man balked at her response. Finally he rasped, "Is this a joke? Are you trying to punish me?"

"I don't understand," she said, frowning. "Why would I punish you?"

"Why are you pretending not to know me?" he demanded.

"I'm not pretending," she cried. "I don't know who *I* am, much less who *you* are."

Desmond gazed at her in disbelief for a moment. "Why, you're Rebecca McCaskie, and I'm Desmond, of course."

Her name didn't mean anything to her, nor did his, and

that knowledge was another cruel disappointment. She had been so sure that the pieces of the puzzle would fall into place once she had some solid clues. "I can't remember you. I have amnesia," she said hurriedly, trying to make some sense of this puzzling confrontation. "How do I know you?" She held her breath and tried to still the frantic hammering of her heart. His response to the question was desperately important to her, and she was almost afraid to hear it. She felt her knees weaken as she waited for him to speak.

He was taken aback for a moment. He glared at her in shocked silence, and a deep crease marred his smooth forehead as his fingers tightened on her shoulders. "What? What did you say? I'm afraid I don't understand. Amnesia? You have *amnesia?* You *really* don't know who I am?"

"I'm sorry," she murmured, miserable because the sight of him had not awakened any response in her, though she was desperately anxious to discover what he knew about her. "There was a car accident, and I bumped my head. I can't remember anything."

Summer watched the crease smooth out and a light begin to glow in his eyes. "Anything? You don't remember what happened a week ago Sunday?"

She shook her head as she studied his expression. Was that relief she saw on his face? "No, I don't."

"You showed up suddenly at my apartment. We—we quarreled." He studied her face carefully, and Summer thought that he was looking for a sign that she remembered the event. "Do you recall that?"

She shook her head again, feeling the beginning of a painful headache. She didn't know who he was, and what was worse, if he was her husband, she didn't want to know. She fought to suppress the awful admission, even from herself. "Did I arrive in a rented car?"

"I don't know," he said. "You ran out of the house, and

I followed you, but you had disappeared before I could catch you. I don't know how you arrived or how you left. I searched everywhere. You left your overnight bag on the front step, and you dropped your purse on the walk. I was positive you would come back, but you never did. I've been sick with worry!"

"If you looked everywhere for me, why didn't you notify the police?" Summer demanded suddenly. "They've been trying to find out who I am, but no one has looked for me."

His face reddened a little. "I was afraid you wouldn't want to see me, darling."

Summer winced at the endearment. She had to know what her relationship was to this man. "Are we married?" she barely whispered.

"Married? No, my precious. We're to be married in the summer—June." He looked deep into her eyes. "I hope we still can be. I hope the . . .the quarrel hasn't changed that."

Summer was faint with the tremendous relief she experienced on hearing that she was only his fiancée, and immediately she was ashamed of herself. She must once have loved this man to have become engaged to him, but all she could think of now was how much she loved Bracken. She pressed trembling fingers to her temples and shivered at the thought.

"You're shaking. This must be awful for you," he said, pulling her close.

Summer drew back, unwilling to be embraced by him. She flushed with guilt when she saw a hurt look cross his face. "I'm sorry," she apologized quickly. "It's just that it's all such a shock to me. I still don't even know who I am, where my family is, what my world consists of. I don't know anything. It's all so confusing."

"Nothing?" he questioned incredulously.

"Nothing," she repeated, then she felt Rose's arm slip protectively around her waist. She had completely forgotten that the woman was standing there, listening to the drama unfold, and she took immense comfort in her touch.

"Do you want to find some place to sit down, Summer?" Rose asked.

"Yes. Yes, of course she does," Desmond exclaimed as though it was an unforgivable oversight on his part. "You look pale as a ghost, Ree. This ordeal is too much for you. Come into the café."

Summer didn't really want to, but she had to find out all she could now. Her future might be standing here before her; she breathed another sigh of relief that she wasn't already married to this man.

"What about my family?" she asked.

He glanced at her uncertainly. "We'll get to that. Come on inside."

"Who does the gold ring belong to?" she asked, watching his expression curiously as he opened the door for her.

He stared vacantly at her. "I beg your pardon. The gold ring?"

"Yes. When I had the accident I was driving a car rented by someone named Ellen Story, and I had a gold band clutched in my hand."

He shook his head. "I don't know. What did it look like?" He pulled out a chair for Summer at an empty table. A nearby waitress was cleaning up the coffee he had spilled earlier.

"It's very wide and has a chainlike design."

Summer was sure he blushed. "Oh. You must have gotten it for me. I didn't know . . . I wasn't aware you had purchased it. You see," he leaned closer and involuntarily Summer sat back in her chair, "you see, you came by my house unexpectedly to surprise me. We had talked of buying rings, but I . . . I hadn't purchased yours yet. I haven't had the money . . . er . . . for the one I want you to have."

Summer looked at him expectantly, but he said nothing more. "Well, tell me," she prompted excitedly. "Who am I? What about my family? Who is Ellen Story? Do I live here in Monterey?"

He laughed lightly. "No, *I* live here. It's an odd coincidence, but you lived with your father in Monterrey, Mexico. He was an administrator in a steel mill there."

Summer felt her heart begin to pound harder. "Was?"

Desmond took her hand in his. "He was killed in an accident two weeks ago. When Ellen and I returned to the States, you stayed on in Monterrey to make the final arrangements for him."

Summer felt the frantic beating of her heart at the thought of her father's death. She had a sinking feeling deep inside, and yet she couldn't recall anything about him. "He had brown eyes, didn't he?" she whispered.

Desmond nodded solemnly.

"Where are my other relatives? Who is Ellen?"

Desmond looked at Rose inquiringly, as if to ask how much he should tell this small, white-faced, tight-lipped, trembling girl who sat beside him. "Ellen is your best friend, and she's out of the country right now. There is no one else; that's why no one looked for you, Ree. But I'm here, darling," he added quickly. "And I do love you, Ree, no matter what you've thought in the past."

She didn't remember what she had thought in the past, and she already had too many terrifying questions to ask him to consider that one now.

A waitress walked up to the table, and Summer jumped.

"Coffee, please," Desmond said. He looked at Summer and Rose, then back at the waitress. "For each of us."

Summer ran shaking hands through her hair. Her

insides were quivering violently. "Why were you in Monterrey? How do I know you? How do I know Ellen Story? How much do you know about me? Oh, dear," she moaned, tears rising to her eyes. "Oh, dear. This is so awful. I still don't remember anything."

As Desmond looked at her, Summer saw compassion in his eyes for the first time. She didn't know whether to be relieved or despairing that he was moved by her plight, that he actually did care for her. She wanted to run home to Bracken and sob her heart out. Bracken was the man she wanted. She felt nothing for this blond intruder who had plagued her memories so. She wanted to be held and comforted by Bracken, the man she knew she loved, but she had no right to seek solace in his arms. Bracken's memories were of a dead wife, and his future was with Darlene Draper.

Desmond stroked her hand affectionately, and she fought an impulse to pull it away. "Ree, you're going to be all right. My darling, I'm so glad I found you. It was fate."

"My father," she murmured. "What do you know about him? About me?"

He stared at her intently for a moment. "Come on, darling," he said. "Let's get out of here. This is no place to talk; we'll go to my apartment."

Summer stood up, stiff and silent, and Rose stood with her. Desmond dropped some money on the table, then brushed past the annoyed waitress, who was approaching with the three cups of coffee.

"We'll go in my car," Desmond said. "I'll drive you back here later."

Rose and Summer followed him to a new compact car. Rose climbed in back, and Summer got in front beside Desmond. He kept looking at her, even when he had started the car and was driving down a winding road to his apartment. Summer stared up at the building, but, like everything else, she had no memory of it. How bitterly ironic, she thought, that she had actually remembered that she lived in Monterey, but she had had the wrong country!

Opening the door, Desmond helped both of them from the car. They walked with him into a very modern apartment. He indicated a blue couch, then asked what they wanted to drink. Rose asked for a glass of iced tea, but Summer shook her head, declining his offer.

"But you must have something," he insisted. "You need a drink. I'll fix your favorite."

Summer did not respond.

"Don't you remember? No. No, of course not, if you don't remember anything," he muttered more to himself than to her. "A pink lady. You always liked a pink lady because it's so mild."

It meant nothing to Summer, but she was numb anyway. She had no one, no one but this blond man who she couldn't remember. A faint hope stayed in her heart that she might remember Ellen Story, but she didn't know why she should when she couldn't even remember her fiancé. Her fiancé! Bracken, her heart cried. Bracken! He was the man who held her heart; it seemed incredible that she had known him only a few days, but she knew she would love him as much if it had been only a few hours. She couldn't be in love with this tall stranger. She couldn't! If she truly loved him, how could she have forgotten him so completely? But then, she must have loved her father, and she didn't remember him either. The tears built up behind her eyes, and she clenched her hands in frustration.

Desmond handed the women their drinks, then seated himself beside Summer. "I can't begin to tell you how relieved I am at finding you."

She gave him no answer, and he rushed on. "Well, let's start at the beginning. About you: I met you at the University of Nuevo León. That's where the city of Monterrey is, in the state of Nuevo León." He paused to see if anything registered. "You, Ellen, and I were students—all in our last year when we met. I fell in love with you, of course, and we began to plan our marriage."

Summer winced at the way he said he had fallen in love with her, "of course." It sounded so cut and dried, so automatic and unemotional. "We were all interested in Mexican history and Mexican artifacts. That's why we all returned to Monterey, California, where my family lived, even though you're from Texas, and Ellen is from Arizona."

Summer twined her fingers together nervously, trying to make some sense of the stream of facts that seemed to have no bearing whatsoever on her life. She could recall nothing, and the pieces of the puzzle didn't seem to fit together for her. "Why?" she asked.

"We've opened a curio shop, darling. Ellen is returning from Europe tomorrow, where she's been picking up odds and ends, vases, statues, and such." He beamed at Summer. "I opened the shop on Wednesday, and already it's attracting business."

"I'm happy for you," she said automatically. His shop meant nothing to her. *He* meant nothing to her. Ellen meant nothing to her. Only Bracken was important.

"But it's for you, too, Ree." He stared at her. "Oh, I'm sorry. This is all too much for you. We've got to take things nice and easy. It will all come back to you. You've suffered a terrible shock, with your father's death and all." He moved nearer to her on the couch and patted her leg. "Drink your drink, darling. Then tell me what you remember about the accident—about anything."

Obediently, Summer took a sip, but she could tell him very little. "I crashed into a man's car on a winding road in Big Sur. I had no identification and no memory of anything. I was in a rented car, so at first the police thought I was Ellen Story. But, when they checked with the landlady, they realized that I wasn't Ellen." Summer felt her lips tremble, and there was an aching emptiness inside her. "Apparently I got the rented car from Ellen. I don't know how or when or why."

Desmond looked down at his maroon slacks. "I see, I see. You probably took her to the airport. She had rented the car the first day she arrived, although I had told her she could use my car. She intends to buy a car when she returns, but she probably told you to use the rented one. You were supposed to stay in her apartment. I didn't know you had come, you see. I spoke with you on Saturday night, and you were still in Texas. You weren't scheduled to arrive until Monday morning." He lowered his voice. "Your father was buried in Texas. I wanted to be with you, but I had to be here—for the business, you know," he added quickly.

Summer shook her head, wondering how she could even have liked him, much less been in love with him. He didn't seem like a very compassionate person. If her father had just died, couldn't Desmond have postponed the opening of the new business for another week?

"I see," she murmured, but she didn't see at all.

Taking her hand in his, he said perceptively, "I don't think you do, darling. We couldn't delay the opening of the business. I had already put ads in the papers, announcements had been made; there were commitments. The building had been leased and stocked. You had made a large investment."

"I had?"

"Yes. Your share was the largest. You're . . .you're quite well off, sweetness. Especially now, I mean, with your father dead."

Summer stared at her hands. The news only made her terribly sad. She had felt better knowing nothing of all this. She wanted to run home and crawl into the bed under the skylight and try to sort out the facts. She didn't feel like a woman with money and a business—and a fiancé.

She wanted to walk in the forest or lie by the stream and sleep.

"Oh, my poor darling," Desmond said in a husky voice, pulling her into his arms and holding her close. Summer remained rigid while he stroked her hair. Determinedly, she kept the tears from falling from her eyes, but her heart wept bitterly at the revelations Desmond had made.

She turned when she heard Rose's stern voice. "I think we'd best be getting back to Isolation now, Miss. You'll be needing time to think this all out. You're in a state now, that's obvious. Mr. Bo might have to call in a doctor to look at you. I think you've heard quite enough for now." Putting her hand firmly on Summer's shoulder, she coaxed, "Come along home."

Gratefully, Summer pulled out of Desmond's arms and stood up.

"You can't leave!" he exclaimed, jumping up. "You'll stay here with me, of course, until Ellen returns. We have so much to talk about."

"You can call for her at the house after she's had time to rest and adjust to all you've told her," Rose said with a hint of iron in her voice. She appeared very formidable if one didn't know her.

Desmond looked puzzled for a moment, unsure whether he should listen to Rose or demand that Summer stay. "What house?" he asked at last.

"Bracken Bohannon's, in Big Sur," Rose said. "It's called Isolation. Just ask anyone when you get to Big Sur. Anybody can tell you where it is." She turned away from him, ready to leave. "If you'll drive us back to our car," she said over her shoulder, taking Summer in hand, "we'll be on our way."

"Wait! Now just a minute here," he insisted, finding his strength. "I think Ree should stay here." His forehead creased. "You say Bracken Bohannon, the novelist?"

Rose nodded.

"Why there?"

"He's the man I ran into," Summer said wearily.

Desmond seemed to see some possibilities in the name that were foreign to Summer, and she hadn't the energy or the inclination to try to figure them out. She wanted nothing more than to return to Isolation and lie down on her bed.

"Here," Desmond said, handing Rose a pencil and paper. "Write down the phone number for me. I can't just let Ree vanish again." He ran his hands through his hair. "This is as confusing to me as it is to everyone else. She disappeared into thin air, and now she doesn't know me. It's quite a shock."

Rose scribbled down the number and handed it to Desmond. He tucked it in his shirt pocket and opened the front door for them. None of them broke the silence as they drove back to the restaurant, but Desmond kept looking over at Summer, who sat very still and stared straight ahead.

When he walked them back to their car, he wrapped his arm around Summer's shoulders. "I'll call you tonight, darling. Rest, and we'll talk about all this later. All right?"

"Yes, Desmond," she agreed, the name feeling strange on her lips.

He turned to face her as they reached the car. "Ree, you can't have forgotten me completely. I won't let you forget me. We're very much in love." He paused again. "We quarreled, darling, don't forget that. But we love each other. We're going to be married in June."

Summer licked her lips nervously, searching for her voice, but it wasn't there.

"Darling?"

"Yes," she said in a hoarse voice. "Yes, I won't forget."

"Good." Bending his head, he placed his warm lips against hers, but Summer couldn't respond. She didn't want his kiss. She knew in her heart of hearts that Bracken

Bohannon was the only man she wanted. But where did she go from here?

Desmond opened the car door for her, and Summer stepped inside. Rose gave a sharp look and, not even waiting for Desmond to say goodby, threw the car into gear and drove off. Summer didn't know how tense she was until they were back on the road to Big Sur and a sigh shuddered through her body.

"You okay?" Rose asked.

"I think so," she replied, but she didn't really know if she would ever be okay again.

Rose looked at her for a moment. "I think we'll just go back to the doctor's office and tell him what's happened," she declared. "I think you should have something to make you sleep tonight."

Without waiting for Summer to comment, Rose turned the car around.

Chapter Ten

The minute Rose stopped the car in front of Isolation, Summer ran for the house. Opening the front door, she rushed inside with every intention of running up to her room, but Bracken caught her in the living room.

"What's wrong?" he demanded. "You look as though you're being chased by demons."

Summer thought that was as accurate a description as she was ever likely to hear. She looked up into the rugged face that she loved so well, and then wrapped her arms around Bracken's broad back, clinging to him.

Lifting her gently in his arms, Bracken, with Rose following close behind, carried Summer up the steps to her room and laid her on the bed.

"What's wrong? What's this all about?" he asked, turning troubled eyes to Rose.

"She met Desmond today," Rose said, as though that statement explained everything. Leaving Bracken to stare after her, she turned on her heel and went to get a glass of water for Summer.

When she was gone, Bracken coaxed the story from Summer while she sat up in bed, pale and trembling.

For a long moment he said nothing. Then he forced a grim smile to his lips. "But, Summer, this is what you wanted," he said in a deep voice. "Now you know who you are, where you belong—who the blond man is, and who the ring belongs to. You can start living again."

Summer shook inside, realizing that her worst fears were coming true. He didn't care. He didn't want her. Now that she had an identity, he could be free of her. She had been an inconvenience, a sexual attraction who resembled his wife.

"Rebecca McCaskie," she corrected with quiet dignity.

"What?" he murmured absently, staring out the window at the pounding surf.

"My name is Rebecca McCaskie. You're still calling me Summer."

His smile was gentle and bittersweet. "You'll always be Summer to me."

Summer fought back a fresh surge of tears. He didn't even want to know Rebecca McCaskie. The girl who had crashed into his car and spent a week and a day in his house, and in his arms, would always be the girl he and the doctor had called Summer, then had forgotten about.

Rose returned with the water, handed Summer a sedative, and sat down on the edge of the bed while she took it.

Mercifully, it was only minutes before Summer drifted into a deep, numbing sleep.

She opened her eyes and blinked at the sun shining through the skylight. The bright ball of yellow was high in the sky. She must have slept for a long, long time. She ran her tongue around her mouth, tasting a bitterness, but that bitterness was nothing like the one that rushed to her mind. Bracken didn't want her. Without so much as one thought for her, he was ready to turn her over to another man—a complete stranger. A man she couldn't even remember. Soon she would have to go away from Isolation, the refuge she loved so dearly. She would have to leave the only man she would ever care for. She turned her head to stare out at the blue expanse of the ocean, and to her surprise she saw Bracken, perched on the windowsill watching her thoughtfully.

Automatically, her heart filled with love for him, and she smiled.

"Good morning."

Summer was both pleased and sorrowful at the warmth in his voice. He showed no regret at the prospect of turning her over to Desmond.

"Are you feeling better?"

She raised a hand to smooth down her wayward hair. "Like a ton of lead fell on me." She tried to sit up in bed, and she was surprised to see that she was in the familiar tee shirt. She frowned. "How did I get into this? I don't remember undressing?"

He grinned. "You didn't. I undressed you."

"You shouldn't have!" she cried indignantly.

The grin broadened. "I didn't mind; it was no trouble."

That hadn't been what she meant, and he knew it. She looked at him sharply, then sighed. What did it matter? He had seen her naked before, though he never would again.

"Your young man called last night," he said soberly.

Summer looked at him. "Oh?"

"Yes. I had Rose tell him you were sleeping. He phoned again this morning, but you were still asleep."

For some silly reason, Summer brightened because Bracken hadn't awakened her. But the feeling was short-lived.

"He's coming over at one to join us for lunch."

Summer drew a deep breath and let it escape through quivering lips. "I suppose it's all for the best. We are engaged, you know."

"Yes, you told me."

"What time is it?" She wondered how much time she had left with Bracken.

"It's twelve-thirty. I came in to wake you. You must be very hungry, since you've missed several meals."

"Yes, I am hungry," she agreed, but she hadn't really noticed if she was or not. How could she think of food when her whole reason for being was vanishing with the passing of time?

"I'll leave you so you can get dressed," he said. "See you downstairs."

Summer watched him leave the room, then she forced herself to get up and take a shower. A few minutes later, she went downstairs.

It was several minutes before she heard the doorbell ring. Bracken strolled to the door to answer it, and, to Summer's chagrin, he invited Desmond into the living room.

Desmond had Summer's purse in his hand, and she accepted it, not even looking at its contents before she laid it on the coffee table. Awkwardly, she began to make the introductions. "Bracken Bohannon, this is Desmond . . . Desmond . . ." To her embarrassment, she didn't even know his last name.

"Mulvaney," he filled in, more than a little agitated.

"May I offer you a drink, Mr. Mulvaney?" Bracken asked, and Summer couldn't help but notice the way Bracken's eyes coldly measured Desmond.

"It's Desmond, and yes, I'd like a scotch and soda." He walked toward the couch with what Summer considered to be cocky confidence and sat down, uninvited.

Bracken nodded. "So you're Summer's fiancé," he said

pointedly, getting to the crucial topic without delay. Desmond nodded, then broke into a monologue about the confusing situation and how it affected them all.

Rose came in to announce that lunch was on the table, and the three of them filed into the dining room. Lunch was as pleasant as could be expected under the circumstances, and Summer was surprised to find that Bracken fairly pumped Desmond for information about her, weighing each small fact carefully before he went on to the next. She learned more about herself from the answers to his pertinent questions than she had learned yesterday, but then, he hadn't been concerned with his heart as she had been with hers. She hadn't even realized that she had forgotten to ask about her age until Desmond told Bracken that she was twenty-two.

When lunch was finished, Desmond insisted on taking Summer to Monterey to see the shop. She made a motion to refuse, but when she looked at Bracken, she saw a frigid expression on his face. Sighing in resignation, she supposed that she had little choice but to go. After all, she didn't see how she could possibly go through with the marriage to Desmond, and she would need to keep busy somehow. The shop might eventually interest her, and she would need something to fill in her lonely hours away from Bracken.

Alone with Desmond in the car for the first time, Summer could come up with little in the way of pleasant conversation. Desmond talked about the shop and how she had been interested in this particular object or that, but Summer had to force herself to listen.

Desmond proudly parked the car in a little neighborhood shopping center parking lot and escorted her to a row of modern buildings, all with dark wood facings. He opened the door for her, and they stepped inside to find a tall red-headed woman standing on a stepladder, strategically placing a long-legged statue on a high shelf.

"Desmond, is that you?" she asked over her shoulder, barely turning her head. "I've been trying to call you." She turned in surprise when she noticed his companion. "Ree!" she exclaimed. "It's wonderful to see you, but where have you been staying? I thought you would be in my apartment when I got back home. Your trunks had been shipped from Mexico to the apartment, and the landlady has been holding them for me."

"It's such an incredible story that you won't believe it," Desmond interjected.

"I have a lot to tell you about the marvelous pieces I purchased in Europe, Desmond," the woman said, "but first I have to hear about Ree. What happened?" she said, looking at Summer with curious green eyes.

Summer stared at her. She was obviously Ellen Story, but like the other face that went with a name she had remembered, Summer didn't know this woman.

Desmond couldn't stand the suspense. "She has amnesia! Can you imagine that? She doesn't know us! She doesn't know anything. It's unbelievable, but she crashed into Bracken Bohannon's car, and she's been staying at his house!"

"What?" Ellen asked, incredulous. "What? Repeat that for me."

"It's true," Summer said quietly. "I'm sorry, but I don't remember you."

"Ree, I can't believe it!" Ellen exclaimed. "For the past year we've been as close as sisters."

Summer gave a slight smile. "I'm afraid I don't remember. I really am sorry. This is so horribly embarrassing. I just don't remember. The doctor says my memory is sure to return, and I've had glimpses of things, but nothing that ties in. I saw Desmond's face and finally remembered a name to go with it, but other than a dark woman that I somehow connect with him, there's been almost nothing to tie me in with my past."

Ellen climbed down off her ladder and walked over to Summer. "You poor dear," she murmured. She looked at Desmond suspiciously for a few brief seconds, then wrapped her arms around Summer. "You will remember; I'm sure of it. You've had some traumas recently, but we'll help you remember."

Summer sensed sympathy and warmth in Ellen, and for some reason she believed that this woman could help her remember, *would* help her to do so.

"Now you just sit down," Ellen insisted, dragging over an old chair, "and tell me about it. It's so hard to believe. I've heard about such cases, but they always seem to happen to other people."

The last thing Summer wanted to do was to go through the awful story again, but she felt she owed it to this friend of hers to explain all that had happened. She repeated the story as quickly as possible, then fell silent.

"Well, you're not to worry your pretty little head about a thing," Ellen insisted confidently. "We'll get you settled in at my place and put you to work in the shop, and before you know it, things will fall into place. I have complete faith, but it *is* an extraordinary story," she mused, looking at Desmond. "As a matter of fact, let's leave Desmond to mind the store, and I'll show you our home right now. It was in our plans you know. Well, you don't remember," she amended, "but it was."

Retrieving her purse from the counter, Ellen blew Desmond a kiss and walked toward the door.

"You take good care of our girl," he instructed, smiling at Summer. "I don't want to lose her again. I don't think I could live through it a second time."

Summer cringed at his words. She didn't want him to care so deeply for her. She was relieved when they were out the door.

Ellen smiled warmly at her. "I can just imagine your relief at seeing Desmond and finding out that he knew you," she said. "It must be dreadful not to know who you are."

"Tell me about Desmond," Summer said. "Was I very much in love with him?" She was as surprised as Ellen that she had actually asked that question, but she had to know the answer. She had no real right to ask it of this girl she didn't even remember, but Ellen *had* said that they had been as close as sisters.

Ellen looked at her speculatively, and Summer was relieved when she spoke. "Why, Ree, how awful not to know if you really loved someone."

Summer's eyes met Ellen's. "Do you know, Ellen? Was I?"

Ellen laughed lightly, breaking the tension. "I hate to say. I don't want to color your relationship, but I see how awkward your position is."

"No, you don't," Summer said quietly, stopping to hold the tall girl's gaze. "You don't see. You couldn't possibly. I've fallen in love with Bracken Bohannon, and I can't bear it when Desmond touches me."

"Ree!" Ellen cried, her hand raising to muffle her words. "Ree, you aren't serious."

Summer's laugh was short and bitter. "Oh, but I am." She hastened to answer the questioning look in the redhead's eyes. "No, Bracken doesn't know. No one knows—except," she added bitterly, "perhaps his mistress."

"My word, how much more confusing can this situation get?" Ellen cried.

"I have to know the answer to my question, Ellen."

"Yes, of course you do," Ellen agreed, starting toward the car again. She waited until they were inside, then she fumbled with the answer. "You must have loved Desmond enough to agree to marriage at some time," she answered thoughtfully, "but you kept postponing it, and Desmond kept pressing you to either marry him or give in to him.

You see," she studied Summer's face, "Desmond considered you quite old-fashioned—a snow princess, he often called you."

"Me?" Summer gasped. "Are you positive? Why, I thought . . . I thought . . ." Her face turned crimson; she was ashamed to admit what she had thought.

"You thought what?" Ellen persisted.

Summer giggled nervously. "I had an idea running around in my head for days that I was some kind of playgirl—a party girl."

Ellen's laughter was sparkling and genuine. "Never! I don't know whatever inspired such a notion. You have a lot to learn about yourself."

"Apparently," Summer agreed, shaking her head, no small amount of relief flooding through her.

"Still, you are in quite a dilemma," Ellen mused. "You need time to work this out, and it sounds pretty complex to me."

Summer nodded, happy to find such a helpful friend, even if she couldn't remember her. She could understand why she had chosen this woman as a companion, and by the time they reached the apartment, Ellen was trying to think of some way to make the transition less painful for Summer. But it seemed futile.

"We'll just move you right in here," she said, opening the door to a cozy upstairs four-room apartment. "I hope you like it."

"I'm sure I will," Summer said, but the thought of leaving Isolation caused her heart to pound.

"Do you have anything to pick up at that writer's house?" Ellen asked. "No, I wouldn't suppose so," she said in answer to her own question. "I guess this is home from today on, though I'm afraid your bedroom may be a little cramped. You only planned to stay with me until June, of course, when you were to marry Desmond, so I didn't give a lot of thought to your room being small. I intended to use it as a storage room when you left."

"I'm sure it will be fine," Summer said. "I'll move in tomorrow. I do have a few things at Bracken's house that I want to pick up, and I want to spend this last night there."

"Of course," Ellen said quickly, but Summer wasn't at all sure that the woman thought it was a good idea. "Let me show you the place, and then I'll drive you back there myself."

"Fine." Summer toured all the rooms, and she had to admit that the apartment was just like something she would have chosen for herself. Though her bedroom was small, it was feminine-looking and thoughtfully decorated. The eat-in kitchen was bright and cheerful, and the living room was enchanting, with large pillows and art objects scattered throughout.

"Have you had lunch?" Ellen asked.

Summer nodded. "Desmond and I ate at Bracken's house."

"Let me take a minute to make a sandwich for myself," Ellen said. "I just flew in an hour ago, and I went right to the shop to hunt for Desmond, even though it's closed for two hours at lunchtime. He wasn't there, of course. Oh, never mind the shop talk," she said, waving a hand. "We'll have plenty of time to talk shop when your situation begins to smooth out. You poor thing. I can't even imagine how distressing this must be for you. How devastating to lose one's memory." She shook her head as she went into the kitchen.

After she had eaten, she drove Summer back to Isolation. She declined Summer's invitation to come in; obviously she didn't have Desmond's interest in the famous writer. She scribbled the apartment and shop phone numbers on a piece of paper.

"Call me when you want me to come for you tomorrow.

And, Ree," she added solemnly. "I'm sure things will work out for you. Try not to be unhappy."

"Thanks, Ellen." Summer smiled, then hurried inside. She felt desolate, thinking that this would be her last night ever in Isolation, her last night in Bracken's company, in his arms. She opened the door and stepped inside. She was surprised to see Bracken lounging on the couch, a tall, frosted drink in his hand.

"Well," he said sharply, "how was your outing with your fiancé?"

Summer was pained by his curt manner. Perhaps he had hoped that she wouldn't return to the house at all, but he must have known she would want the few possessions she had there. Or did he think she should leave them since he had paid for them, and she hadn't typed enough to repay him.

"It was fine," she replied defiantly. "Quite pleasant."

"I've no doubt," he said with a bitter laugh. He took another long drink from the glass, and Summer could only surmise that he must have been sitting there reminiscing about Marissa. What else would account for his surly disposition?

"So," he said, "my little unknown waif is the proprietress of a shop and an heiress."

Summer studied him for a moment before she decided that she didn't want to listen to him when he was in this mood. This was the Bracken of old, bitter and snarling. She was surprised to realize that over the days she had known him, he had mellowed somewhat. Shaking her head, puzzled over his unpleasant manner, she walked to the stairs and went up to her room.

It was quite apparent that there was nothing left for her here. Bracken had never wanted anything more from her than a cheap fling, and she had almost given in to him, in fact, would have given in to him at least at one point. The foolish dreams she had harbored of a future with him were never to be. Walking to the closet, she yanked the clothes he had bought her from the hangers and laid them out on the bed. Then she took out the items that belonged to Rose. She would have to return those after dinner and ask for something in which to take the other clothes to Ellen's apartment. She was folding a pair of jeans when Bracken appeared in the doorway.

"What are you doing?" he demanded.

Summer tossed the jeans down on the bed. So! He *didn't* want her to take the things. She couldn't imagine what he expected to do with them. Perhaps it was principle with him. She hadn't paid for them, and therefore she wasn't entitled to take them.

"I was packing," she answered tartly, "but perhaps you believe that I have no right to these clothes since I didn't pay for them."

"I don't care what you do with the clothes," he growled, coming into the room. "You obviously can't wait to get out of here. It was haven enough when you had no other place to go, but I see that, true to your word, once you've found Desmond again, you're eager to leave."

Summer stared at him wide-eyed for a moment. "I—that isn't it," she murmured.

"Spare me," he snapped. "Rose has dinner ready. Come and eat."

With that comment he whirled away from her and strode out of the room. Summer was left to stare after him, perplexed. Could he possibly want her to stay with him in Isolation? No, of course not.

She left the clothes lying on the bed and walked slowly down to the dining room. Dinner was on the table, and Summer sat down. Instead of attempting to make her last evening with him pleasant, she found that Bracken was sullen and unwilling to discuss her future. He hardly spoke to her at all. Bitterly disappointed, she ate very little of the food and excused herself. Bracken didn't even glance at her as she left the table.

She went into the kitchen where Rose and Harry were eating. When they invited her to sit down, she told Rose that she needed something to pack her few clothes in and that she would bring down the clothes Rose had lent her.

"Are you leaving?" Rose asked.

Summer nodded.

"Well, I don't want the clothes back that I gave you. I've got no use for them. Take them if you want. Soon's I finish eating, I'll find a bag for your things."

"Thanks, Rose." Summer turned away and went up to her room. When Rose brought up a small suitcase a little later, she packed her clothes, then retired early. She was lying in bed reading Bracken's first book when a sudden hard rain came up. She stared up at the large raindrops pounding down on the skylight. The rain was soothing and romantic, she thought distractedly, then she turned back to the book. It was good, as Bracken had said, but his inexperience did show. She thought about the story, trying to keep from dwelling on her own unhappy plight. She had cried over it until there were no more tears left in her. She had to resign herself to her fate. She should consider herself fortunate that she had learned her identity and that she was not without friends or money. She should consider herself lucky, even though she couldn't have the one thing she wanted. She would spent her future reliving the memories of the time she had shared with Bracken, and wishing that things had worked out differently.

Summer spent a restless night, and she awakened just as night was yielding to day. Bracken wasn't up when she went down to breakfast, and she quickly ate the bacon and eggs Rose served her, promising herself that she would take one last walk in the forest before leaving Isolation. She hoped to find some strength in the tall trees and peaceful surroundings; then she would thank Bracken for his hospitality and leave him and his home forever.

"Devil!" she called when she had taken the last bite of her breakfast. "Devil, come on. Let's go for a walk."

Rose entered with the panting dog. "Are you going out into the forest?" she asked.

"Yes, I'd like to take one last walk before I leave."

"Be careful," Rose warned. "It's barely light now, and it poured last night."

"I know," Summer said. "I watched it fall on my skylight. It was so soothing."

"Now, don't you go and get lost this time," Rose said sharply. "You stay on the trail, and you keep the house in sight, you hear me?"

Summer smiled, thinking of the last time she had gone into the forest. "Don't worry, Rose. I don't want to suffer the same fate as before. I'll be careful, and I won't be gone more than thirty minutes. It's just so quiet in the woods, and I'd like to sort out my life before I leave."

Rose nodded knowingly, then watched as Summer went up for a jacket. In minutes the girl was striding down the trail with Devil galloping alongside.

Summer was surprised by the fog when she went deeper into the forest. She knew she would have to be very careful this morning if she was to keep from losing her way. She turned back to look at the house, seeing that it was still in sight. When she rounded a section of trees, a small animal darted out of the thicket. Spying the game, Devil charged after it.

"Come back here, Devil!" Summer ordered, but Devil had a mind of his own, and, his prey in sight, he plunged into the damp forest.

"Oh dear!" Summer cried impatiently, seeing what she had hoped would be a soothing, restorative walk turn into a contest as she ran after Devil. She was afraid of losing him in the mist, and she didn't want to have to explain to

Bracken that she had taken the dog for a walk and that he had disappeared.

Barely able to keep Devil in sight, she ran faster, angrily calling out, "Devil! Devil! You come back here!" Suddenly she encountered a flat stone covered with a soggy mat of dead leaves. Her foot skidded out from under her, and before she could regain her balance, she collided with a tree in her path. Her head hit the trunk with a dull thud. The last thing she remembered was an explosion of pain as she sank to the ground.

Summer was soaked to the bone from the dampness of the forest when, moaning softly, she opened her eyes to find Bracken bending over her, lightly slapping her face with a gentle hand.

"Summer! Summer, are you all right?" he asked, his gray eyes filled with concern.

Holding her head with both hands, Summer sat up and looked dazedly around. Devil was sitting beside her, panting, his head cocked to one side as he watched her.

"Darn you, Devil!" Summer managed to say. She tried to meet Bracken's eyes, but she was embarrassed. "He ran after some animal," she murmured weakly, as if that explained her situation.

"He can take care of himself," Bracken said. "It's you I'm worried about. Now, tell me what happened."

Summer imagined that a lump was already forming on her throbbing forehead. Reaching up, she touched it gently. "I tried to keep up with Devil. I didn't want to lose him in the fog. I kept calling him, but he wouldn't come back. I . . . I guess I slipped on a stone."

"Another fool stunt!" Bracken snapped. "What were you doing out here in this early morning mist?" Kneeling before her, he smoothed back her hair with a surprisingly tender touch as he carefully surveyed her forehead. Summer felt suddenly breathless as Bracken traced her hairline with his finger. "Do you feel all right?" he asked more gently. "Can you stand?"

She experienced a sudden surge of love for him as he gazed at her anxiously. Her lips trembled softly. "I have a slight headache, but I don't think I'm hurt."

A small tremor went through her as Bracken wrapped his arm around her waist and carefully helped her to her feet. Looking down into her eyes, his lips much too near hers, he asked, "Are you sure you're all right? Does anything seem to be damaged?"

Summer's eyes were misty as they met his. She wanted to tell him that she would never be all right again if she couldn't have his love, but she smiled sadly and nodded.

Suddenly Bracken's lips lowered to hers, and he kissed her lingeringly as he pulled her to his chest. When he ended the kiss, he asked huskily, his lips near her ear, "Summer, will you be happy with Desmond?"

"Desmond?" she murmured confusedly. "Desmond!" she cried, pulling back to gaze up into Bracken's eyes. Her hands tightened on his arms as a frown crossed his forehead. "Bracken! I remember! Oh, thank heavens! I remember!"

"What? You remember what?"

"I remember about Desmond! I remember who I am! I remember what happened!"

"Well, don't leave me hanging, woman," Bracken said impatiently.

"I went to Desmond's apartment after I took Ellen to the airport. I wanted to surprise him. And there he was, making love to a dark-haired woman in his living room!" A flush of embarrassment crept up her body as Summer relived the scene in her mind.

"And?" Bracken demanded.

"When he opened the door to answer my knock, I could see the woman on the couch; her clothes were a mess. Desmond didn't have a shirt on. I . . . I lost my temper. I said all kinds of terrible things to him." She frowned at the memory.

"And what did he do?" Bracken growled, his brows meeting in a hard line.

"He was embarrassed, and mad. He called me a snow princess. He said I didn't know how to be a real woman, that what he needed was a party girl, so he had found himself one." Circles of scarlet tainted Summer's cheeks. "The woman on the couch was laughing—at me. I ran away, and I must have dropped my purse enroute. I got in the car, but I didn't know what to do then, so I just drove away not knowing where I was going."

"And you still want to marry that man?" Bracken asked gruffly.

"No!" she cried incredulously. "No! I realized at the restaurant the day I saw him that I didn't love him—and no wonder! I had never been sure of that love, but he kept pressuring me to marry him. He pleaded with me to invest in the curio shop." Memories flooded her mind, pouring forth as if from a fountain. "He even asked me to buy him that expensive gold wedding band. It was a collector's item! What a fool I was for him," she muttered.

Bracken stared at her. "You don't love Desmond? You don't intend to marry him?"

"No!" she cried again. "How could I love Desmond when I'm in love with you?" The words were out before she could contain them.

"Me?" he asked in disbelief. "Me?"

Embarrassed by her outburst, Summer fell silent as she stood gazing up into his face. She lowered her eyes and managed a somewhat uncertain nod.

"That's wonderful!" he exclaimed, grabbing her up in a bear hug and whirling her around.

"It is?" she murmured, looking into his eyes, and forgetting all about her headache in her excitement.

"Of course it is. You don't know how I've hated that

blond man in your past because I didn't know how much you cared for him. I've wanted you for myself since you called me back when you were in the hospital. I wanted to hold you in my arms and tell you not to worry, that I would take care of you, but I didn't know who had a prior claim."

"You wanted me?" she asked, blinking her eyes as he set her back on her feet.

"Wanted you?" he groaned deeply. "I've been wild with wanting you."

"But what about Darlene?"

"What *about* Darlene? I told you she's an old friend. She and Marissa were girlhood chums."

"You don't love her?"

"Darlene?" he asked. "Where on earth would you get that idea?"

"But your mistress—" Summer's words trailed away.

It was Bracken's turn to blink puzzled eyes. "Mistress? Mistress!" he muttered. "You surely didn't think Darlene was my mistress? The mistress Marissa couldn't cope with was my writing. She despised it, and she started seeing other men because she felt she was being neglected. I guess I didn't love her enough to give up my career for her, regardless of her behavior."

"Your writing!" Summer cried. "But I don't understand —but I thought—what about that room you keep just as she left it? You must have cared deeply for her at one time." She lowered her eyes. "And you called out her name that night you spent with me."

Bracken drew a deep breath and let it slip through his lips. "Did I? I think that's the night I finally laid Marissa's ghost to rest." He tilted Summer's chin and gazed deep into her eyes. "I thought I loved Marissa, or I never would have married her. I tried to love her, but she was shallow and superficial. She thought only of herself, and it takes two to love. I guess I've kept her room that way because of the guilt I feel. What a waste of a life. It's agony to think you're responsible for someone's death."

"But you weren't responsible," Summer declared.

"I failed her. I couldn't give her what she thought she needed from me." He shrugged his shoulders. "But that's all past now. I've found something of my own to live for. I've no right to ask you, but will you marry me, Summer?"

"Oh, Bracken," she breathed. "Yes, of course I will."

He bent his head and gently touched her forehead with his lips. "What a lovely bruise," he said softly. "It caused your memory to return."

Summer reached up and pulled his head lower so that their lips met. Wrapping his arms around her, Bracken drew her close to his body as the kiss deepened. When Summer began to tremble, he pulled away.

"You're freezing; your clothes are damp. Let's get back to the house." He reached down and lifted her in his arms, hugging her to his chest. His lips near hers, he murmured, "I'm never going to let you get cold again."

Summer smiled. "I wasn't trembling from the cold, Bracken." Looking at him from beneath lowered lashes, she murmured, "Your touch always does that to me."

He chuckled, then said thoughtfully, "You know, you were right about your name."

"When?"

"When you introduced yourself at the party as Summer Bohannon. That's the name you'll carry the rest of your life, and I hope my touch will always make you tremble."

Summer nestled her head contentedly against his shoulder as he carried her from the forest. All the nightmares of Rebecca McCaskie were left behind her. Summer Bohannon, she told herself wonderingly. A beautiful smile curved her lips; she was going to be Bracken Bohannon's bride!